C000132226

FORGOTTEN GODS

TALES AND LEGENDS OF EGYPTIAN, GREEK, AND NORSE GODS

PIERRE MACEDO

LEIRBAG PRESS

ISBN: 978-0-9959742-4-1
eBook ISBN: 978-0-9959742-5-8

First Edition
First Printing, 2017
10 9 8 7 6 5 4 3 2 1

Leirbag Press
www.leirbagpress.com
contact@leirbagpress.com

Contents

PREFACE

There was a time when the gods were an important part of humankind's life. Men and women worshiped their deities in search of protection, health, good harvests, and everything that was the responsibility of some god. In Ancient Egypt, the Egyptians promoted great festivals, rituals, and ceremonies dedicated to the dozens of gods in their culture, among whom we can highlight Isis, Osiris, Ra, and Horus. In Greece, the Olympian gods played an even more active role on earth. Greek mythology is rich in stories that tell how the gods related to the Greek people, sometimes even talking and passing on their knowledge directly to them. The Norse people greatly valued the inhabitants of the kingdom of Asgard, such as the great Odin, the strong Thor, and the brave Frey, offering them sacrifices in exchange for prosperity, safe travel, among others. These and so many other gods were forgotten with the advent of the Christian era, and their cult was virtually extinct.

This book attempts to rescue the memory of the major Egyptian, Greek and Norse gods through tales and legends that tell their stories and adventures. I encourage you, regardless of your belief, to know better the deities presented here and to understand that they deserve the same respect as any other god worshiped nowadays.

IN SEARCH OF TRUTH

I was born in a Catholic family, not so traditional to be honest, but as a child, we used to go to church on Sunday mornings. I never felt the need to be present in the church, and I always questioned the things that were said by the priests. But even so, there I was fulfilling my Christian obligation.

At the age of 14, I began to prepare for Chrismation, a sacrament of the Catholic Church in which the faithful receive from the bishop an anointing with the Chrism (olive oil). All Catholics must undergo this ritual, and then at the age of 15, I was "Chrismed." What should have been the beginning of a closer bond with the Catholicism, was the beginning of a complete abandonment.

I have always wanted to understand how Jesus Christ and his father can be the only gods of this immense universe if in other beliefs there are dozens of other gods who were worshiped in the past or who still are. How is it possible to affirm the truth of something when our knowledge is limited? The fact is you cannot unless you open your mind and try to understand how things work out of your world.

I confess that the gods that will be addressed in this book were not the first ones I came into contact with after abandoning the Catholicism. At that time, I still doubted anything referred to mythologies, including the Norse, Greek, and Egyptian, but then I discovered that all the gods exist and they are always willing to help those who seek them and believe in them.

I first contacted a Pai-de-Santo (literally "father of the saint"), who is a kind of priest or leader of the Candomblé religion. I told him what my problem was, and he asked the Orixás, the higher spiritual entities of this religion, to help me. I went to his place on a Friday morning, and there the work was done. This ritual with the Orixás included the sacrifice of chickens and offerings of food and drink. What I had requested was not granted, but I soon discovered that the Pai-de-Santo who charged me $ 100.00 for the service was not reliable.

The first ritual I performed dedicated to a deity, was to Frey and Freya, two gods of the Norse mythology. I was facing some personal problems that I could not solve on my own, and I needed some divine assistance. I did not have a suitable place or the knowledge to do a worthy ritual, but for the first time attempting such a thing, the experience was valid for sure. I did not get an immediate response from them, but over time things got better.

Since then, my curiosity to understand more and more these incredible beings only increased, and I never stopped appealing to them in times of need. Because wise is the one who is not bound to dogmas and does not allow their knowledge to be limited by beliefs that try to induce them to believe in a not-so-real reality.

THEY DID NOT ABANDONED US

If we could go back to Ancient Greece in the period between 1100 and 146 BC, we would find that the Greeks were a people that had a deep connection with their religion and worshiped intensely various gods like the great Zeus, Hera, Poseidon, Hades, Aphrodite, Athena, among others. The main forms of worship of that people to their deities included great temples scattered throughout Greece, animal sacrifice and festivals. One of the main festivals was the Afrodisa, dedicated to Aphrodite goddess of love, beauty, and sexuality. On commemoration days, the temples of the goddess were carefully cleaned and decorated, and the altars purified with dove blood, which is her sacred bird. Other celebrations included the Hermaia, Anthesteria, and the

Panathenaia, dedicated to Hermes, Dionysus, and Athena respectively. What remains of all this Greek religious culture are manuscripts, statues, and temple ruins, as well as the name of the capital city of Greece, Athens, which were the center of worship of the goddess Athena.

Almost three thousand kilometers from Greece lies the Nordic region consisting of Denmark, Norway, Sweden and Iceland where was the birthplace of the Vikings who were the most faithful representatives of the Norse gods. Among the many gods of this mythology, we can highlight Odin, Balder, Thor, Loki, and Freya. As a people of warriors who were always involved in battles and territorial disputes, the cult of the Vikings to their deities almost always included animal sacrifices. Some textual and archaeological sources indicate the existence of human sacrifices as well. However, there is a debate whether these were done voluntarily or if they were forced. And due to the scarcity of evidence regarding such practice, it is possible to conclude that human sacrifice was rare and used only on very special occasions.

In Egypt, the period of worship of different deities is even older, dating from 3150-30 BC. Among the dozens of gods recorded in manuscripts, we can emphasize Horus, Ra, Isis, and Osiris. The gods' statues were washed, perfumed and fed daily by the priests and they were locked in the center of the temples that were not open to the public. The cults were based on daily ceremonies, rituals, and festivals with processions in which an image of the god was carried out from the temples. Fortunately, as in Ancient Greece, the Egyptians left several records of their spiritual activities, and the most important ones are located in the Sahara Desert within the magnificent pyramids.

The practices synthesized above decreased over time until their near extinction. We abandoned the gods that had been with us for thousands of years. Christianity and Islam largely replaced polytheistic religions. Currently, approximately 92% of the Greek population is Christian, 90% of the Nordic people are also Christians, and 90% of Egyptians are Muslim. The worship of ancient gods still exists in some parts of the world, but they are very restricted.

TALES OF ASGARD
NORSE GODS

ODIN AND BALDER

The great god Odin was the father of all the gods. He and his children dwelt in the city of Asgard at the end of the rainbow.

Odin's palace was as high as the sky and roofed with pure silver. In it was a throne of gold. When Odin sat upon the throne, he could see all over the world.

Each day he sat upon the throne to see if everything was as it should be on the earth. He loved the people and the animals, and all the beautiful things of the earth because they were the work of his hands.

Odin had two ravens which were as swift as thought. Every day he sent the ravens to fly over the oceans and over the land to see if any harm was being done. When they came back, they perched upon his shoulders and whispered in his ear all that they had seen.

Besides this, there was a watchman who never slept. He was called Heimdal, the white god. He always stayed at the foot of the rainbow, which was the bridge of the gods, to see that the frost giants did not come into Asgard, and to listen to the sounds of earth. So sharp were his ears that he could hear the grass and the wool on the sheep's backs growing.

One day when Odin mounted his throne, he saw that the earth was no longer green and beautiful. The air was full of snowflakes, and the ground was as hard, as iron. All was dark and cold.

The ravens, which had been sent out to see if all was well, came hurrying back to tell Odin that Hoder, the blind old god of darkness, had taken possession of the earth.

Heimdal, the watchman, called that he could, no longer hear the music of the waterfalls and birds, and all the pleasant sounds of earth. Everything was mute with fear of the terrible god of darkness.

Odin called the gods together, and they looked with pity on the great earth, which had been such a pleasant place.

Thor, the strong god, offered to go with his hammer and fight with the god of darkness, but Odin knew that Hoder could hide himself away from Thor.

Then Balder, the Beautiful, the god of light, whom all the gods loved, offered to go. So Odin gave him his winged horse, Sleipner, and he rode away across the rainbow bridge.

As soon as the light of Balder's shining eyes fell upon the poor, cold earth, it brightened and stirred. But the old, blind god Hoder brought all his forces of darkness to resist the god of light, and the earth lay as if dead.

Balder struck no blows as Thor, the strong god, wished to do. He did not even try to resist the god of darkness. He only smiled upon the earth and called to it to awake.

At last, the blind god turned and fled before the light of Balder's face. Then the streams leaped up and sang, and the birds came back, and the flowers bloomed.

Everywhere the grass and the waving grain sprang up beneath Balder's footsteps, and the trees put out their gayest blossoms to greet him.

The squirrels and rabbits came out of the places where they had hidden themselves and danced and frisked with joy. Never had the earth been so beautiful.

But Hoder, the blind god, in his realm of darkness, was only waiting for an opportunity to take possession of the earth again. So Odin permitted Balder's mother to cross the rainbow bridge to help her son.

The goddess went through all the earth, begging each plant and stone and tree not to harm her son, who had brought them nothing but blessings. And every tree and shrub and tiny plant, and every rock and pebble, and every stream and little brook promised gladly. Only the mistletoe, which grows high up in the oak tree and not upon the ground as other plants do, was forgotten.

Loke, who was a meddlesome god, always doing something wrong, found out that the mistletoe had not given the promise, and told Hoder.

Hoder thought that because it was so little and weak, it could not really kill the god. So he shot an arrow tipped with a tiny twig of mistletoe at Balder.

The arrow pierced through and through the beautiful god, and he fell dead. Then the earth put off her green robe and grew silent and dark for a time.

But because Balder, the Beautiful, had once lived on earth, Hoder could only make it cold half the year and dark half the day.

And even now, if you listen, in the winter you can hear the wind moan through the trees which fling their great arms in grief. And on summer mornings very early, you will find the stones and the grass wet with weeping in the darkness.

But when the sun shines the tears are turned to diamonds and the earth is glad, remembering Balder the Good.

> I heard a voice, that cried,
> "Balder the Beautiful is dead! "
> And through the misty air
> Passed like the mournful cry
> Of sunward sailing cranes.
> Balder the Beautiful,
> God of the summer sun,
> Fairest of all the Gods!
> Light from his forehead beamed,
> Runes were upon his tongue,
> As on the warrior's sword.
>
> All things in earth and air
> Bound were by magic spell
> Never to do him harm;
> Even the plants and stones,
> All save the mistletoe,
> The sacred mistletoe!
>
> Hoder, the blind old God,
> Whose feet are shod with silence,
> Pierced through that gentle breast

With his sharp spear by fraud
Made of the mistletoe,
The accursed mistletoe!

FENRIS-WOLF

Loke was a mischievous fellow. He was always getting the other gods into trouble. Sometimes they shut him up. But they always let him out, because he was so cunning that he could help them to do things they could not do for themselves.

Once he crossed the rainbow bridge to Jotunheim, the land of the giants, and brought home a giantess for his wife.

Very strange children Loke had. One of them was the Fenris-wolf. He was named Fenrir. All the gods knew he was a wolf as soon as they saw him. But he went about among the children, playing with them like a good-natured dog, and the gods thought there was no harm in him.

Fenrir grew larger and larger, and the gods began to look at him with distrust. They feared he might someday grow too strong for them. But Fenrir always looked good-natured and harmed no one. He did not even show that he had great strength. So the gods could not have the heart to kill him.

But they put it off too long. One day they found Fenrir had grown so strong that it was almost too late to do anything with him. All the gods worked day and night until they had forged a chain they thought strong enough to bind the wolf.

Knowing they could not bind Fenrir against his will, all the gods came together for games. Thor crushed mountains with his hammer. The other gods showed their strength by lifting and leaping and wrestling.

Then they brought out the chain and told Fenrir to let them bind him with it so that he might show his strength by breaking it.

Fenrir knew that he could break the chain, so he allowed himself to be bound. He only drew in a deep breath, and the chain dropped into pieces.

Then the gods forged a chain twice as strong as the first. Fenrir saw that this chain would be hard to break. But breaking the first chain had made him stronger. So he allowed this one to he put on him.

This, too, he broke, and the gods were in despair. They knew they could never make a stronger chain, and they feared the wolf more than ever.

Odin took his horse, Sleipner, and went on a seven days' journey to the home of the dwarfs. They lived deep down in the earth and had charge of the gold and diamonds and all other precious things. They were the most cunning of blacksmiths.

When Odin told the little people what he wanted, they all cried, "Never fear, Father Odin! We can make a chain that will bind the wolf."

When the chain was made, it was as light and delicate as a spider's web, but Odin knew it could never be broken.

As soon as Fenrir saw the chain, he was afraid of it. He knew if it were only a cobweb they never care to put it on him. So he would not allow himself to be bound unless a god's hand was put into his mouth. At this, the gods only looked one another. After a little time, Tyr, the bravest of all the gods, put his hand into the wolf's mouth.

The moment the chain touched Fenrir, he knew he could never break it, and he bit off the god's hand. But the Fenris-wolf was bound forever.

LOKE

One day Loke was wandering about idly as he often did. He came near Thor's house, which had five hundred and forty rooms.

By the window sat Sif, Thor's wife, asleep. Loke thought it would be a good joke to cut off her beautiful hair and make Thor angry. So he crept in softly and cut off her hair close to her head without wakening her.

When Thor came home and found out what had been done, he knew at once who had done it

Rushing out, he overtook Loke and threatened to crush him to atoms. To save his life, Loke swore to get the elves to make hair of gold for Sif that would grow like real hair.

Loke knew he had better do as he had promised, so he went deep down into the earth to Alfheim. When he came near, he looked through a crevice in the ground, and there were the elves at work. He could see them by the light of the forge fires.

Some were running about with aprons on and with sooty faces. Some were hammering iron, and others were smelting gold. Some were cutting out rock crystals and staining them red for garnets and rubies. The elf women brought violets and the greenest grass to be found on the earth above. With these, they stained crystals blue and green for sapphires and emeralds.

Some of the elf women brought children's tears from the upper earth, and the gentlest elves changed them into pearls.

As fast as they were finished, the jewels were carried away by the little elf boys and hidden in the ground, where they are found to this day. If you wish to see what cunning workmen the elves were, look at the shining faces and straight edges of quartz crystals, or at the beautiful coloring of emeralds and rubies.

The little elf girls crept through the earth under the ocean and gave the pearls to the oysters to keep. Even now the oysters shut their shells tight and will not give up the pearls.

Loke watched the little workmen a long time. Then he went in and told his errand. Nothing delighted the elves so much as to have work to do. They promised Loke the golden hair, and at once began to make it.

A little elf ran in with a handful of gold, and an old grandmother spun it into hair. As she spun, she sang a magic song to give life to the gold. At the same time, the elf blacksmiths and goldsmiths set about making a present for Loke.

The blacksmiths made a spear that would never miss its mark. The goldsmiths made a ship that would sail without wind. Besides, it could be folded up and put into the owner's pocket.

Loke appeared before the gods with these wonderful things. To Odin, he gave the spear, and to Frey the ship. Thor took the golden hair and put it upon Sif's head. Immediately it began to grow. At this, the gods pardoned Loke.

When Loke went out, he began to boast that the sons of Ivakl, who had made the gifts, were the best workmen in the world.

Brok, an elf of another family, heard him, and exclaimed angrily, "Sindre, my brother, is the best blacksmith in the whole world!"

Loke dared Brok to show him three gifts of Sindre's making equal to the spear, the ship, and the hair.

Brok hastened to Sindre and told him. The two brothers began the work at once. Sindre put a pigskin into the furnace and told Brok to blow the fire with the bellows while he went out. Brok worked with a will. Loke had followed him, and now changed himself into a fly and stung Brok's ear. But Brok worked steadily, never stopping to brush it off.

Sindre came back and took out the pigskin, and it had become a golden pig. So bright was it, that it made the cave as light as day.

Then Sindre put a little piece of gold into the furnace and went out again. Again, as Brok worked at the bellows, the fly came and stung him on the nose. But the elf did not stop for an instant.

When Sindre took out the gold, it had become a magic golden ring. From it, every ninth night dropped eight golden rings.

This time Sindre brought a piece of iron and put it into the furnace. Brok began his work. But Loke changed himself into a hornet and stung the elf on the forehead until the blood ran into his eyes.

Brok bore it a long time. Then he paused a moment to drive away the hornet. Just then his brother came in and said it was of no use to go on after he had once stopped.

Sindre took out the iron, and it had become the mighty hammer Mjolner. But the handle was a little too short. This was because the elf had stopped when the hornet stung him.

Brok took the golden pig, the ring, and the hammer to Asgard and presented them to the gods. Thor had just lost his hammer in a great fight with the Midgard Serpent, so Mjolner was given to him. This hammer could never be lost because it would always return to the owner.

The pig, Golden Bristle, was given to the sun god, Frey, because he had to take long journeys in dark places. Odin kept the golden ring himself.

The gods voted Sindre, a better blacksmith than the sons of Ivald. Brok demanded Loke's head, which had been wagered. The cunning Loke said he might have the head, but he must not touch the neck. So the elf did not get the head.

THOR

Thor was the strong god. So strong was he that he could crush mountains with one blow of his hammer.

His eyes shone like fire. When he drove in his chariot, the sound could be heard all over the earth. When he struck with his terrible hammer fire streamed through the sky.

On the one hand he wore an iron glove to grasp the hammer. Around his waist was a belt. Every time he tightened the belt his strength was redoubled.

If he had crossed the rainbow bridge, it would have fallen down. So every day he waded through four rivers to go to the council of the gods.

Thor was usually as good-natured as he was strong. But sometimes he had sudden attacks of anger. Then he drove furiously in his chariot, striking in every direction with his hammer. Sometimes he did damage which, with all his strength, he could never repair.

Very often Thor did kind things. Once the dwarf, Orvandal, did not go into his home in the ground when the frost giants were in the land. They caught him and took him to Jotunheim.

Thor waded across the cold river, Elivagar, to the land of the giants, and brought Orvandal back in a basket. When they were nearly across, Orvandal put one toe outside, and it was bitten off by the frost giants.

Thor liked nothing better than to go on long journeys, seeking adventures. Once he set out in his chariot drawn by goats, and Loke, the cunning, went with him.

Night came. Thor made himself no larger than a man and asked to stay all night in a poor man's hut by the seashore.

The man welcomed them. Thor killed his goats, and the poor man's wife cooked them.

When nothing was left but the bones, Thor told the children to put them all into the skins on the floor. But one of the boys broke a bone to get the marrow.

At dawn the next day, Thor touched the bones with his hammer, and the goats sprang up alive. But one of them was lame. When the family saw the bones changed into living goats, they were very much frightened.

Thor was angry because the goat was lame and grasped his hammer so tightly that his knuckles grew white. At first, he meant to kill the whole family, but after he thought, he only took away two of the children for servants.

They crossed the ocean that day and found a forest on the other side.

When it grew dark, they went into a cave to sleep. In the cave, there were five small rooms and one large one. All night they heard a great rumbling noise.

Early in the morning when they went out, they found an immense giant sleeping on the ground. The noise they had heard was the giant's breathing, and the cave was his glove.

When Thor saw him, he tightened his belt of strength and grasped his hammer. But just then the giant awoke and stood up. His great height so amazed Thor that he forgot to strike and only asked the giant's name.

The giant replied that he was Skrymer. Then he asked to go along with Thor. Thor said he might, and they all sat upon the ground to eat breakfast.

After breakfast, the giant put Thor's provision sack into his own and carried both. All that day he strode in front and Thor followed.

At night they stopped. The giant drank a small brook dry, and at once lay down on the ground and fell asleep.

Thor found that he could not untie the sack. At this, he was very angry.

He tightened his belt and went out where the giant lay. He swung his hammer above his head and struck the giant's forehead with all his strength.

The giant awoke and rubbed his eyes. Then he said sleepily, "I think a leaf must have fallen upon me." With that, he fell asleep again.

Thor and the others lay down without any food, and the giant snored so that they could not sleep.

Again Thor arose. He tightened his belt twice and struck the giant a harder blow than the first. The giant only stirred and muttered, "This must be an oak tree because an acorn has fallen upon my forehead."

Thor hurried away and waited until the giant once more slept soundly. Then he went softly and struck him so hard that the hammer sank into his head.

This time the giant sat up and looked around him. Seeing Thor, he said, "I think there are squirrels in this tree. See, a nutshell has fallen and scratched my forehead."

"But make ready to go now. We are near the palace of Utgard."

"You see how large I am. In Utgard's palace, I am thought small. If you go there, do not boast of your strength."

With that, he directed Thor to the palace and went away northward.

At noon they saw a palace so high that they had to bend back their heads to see the top of it.

The gate was locked. So they crept in through the bars and went from room to room until they came to the hall where sat Utgard with his men around him.

For some time he pretended not to see Thor. Then with a loud laugh, he said, "Ho! Ho! Who is this little creature? " Without waiting for a reply, he cried, " Why, I believe it is Thor of whom we have heard."

Then speaking to Thor for the first time, he said. "Well, little man, what can you do? No one is allowed here unless he can do something."

Loke, who was quicker than Thor, said, "I can eat faster than anyone here." Then Utgard said, "Truly that is something. We will see if you have spoken the truth."

The giants brought in a trough filled with meat. Utgard called Loge, one of his men, to contend with Loke.

Loke and Loge met in the middle of the trough. But Loke had only eaten the meat, while Loge had eaten, meat, bones, and trough. So Loke was beaten.

Then Utgard asked what Thjalfe, the boy Thor had taken from the seashore, could do. Thjalfe replied that he could outrun any man there.

Utgard called a little fellow whose name was Huge. Huge so far outran Thjalfe that he turned back and met him half way.

Utgard said: "You are the best runner that ever came here, but you must run more swiftly to outrun Huge."

Then Thor was asked what he wished to contend. He answered: "In drinking."

Utgard sent the cup bearer to bring his great drinking horn.

When Thor took the horn in his hand, Utgard said: "Most of the men here empty it at one draught. Some empty it at two draughts. But no one ever takes three."

Thor put the horn to his lips and drank deep and long. When he was out of breath, he lowered the horn. To his surprise, very little of the water was gone.

Utgard said: "I should have thought Thor could drink more at a draught."

Thor did not reply but drank again as long as he had any breath. This time enough was gone so that the horn could be carried easily without spilling any of the water.

Utgard said: "Have you not left too much for the third draught?"

Thor became angry. He put the horn to his lips and drank until his head swam, and his ears rang, and fire floated before his eyes.

But the horn was not nearly empty, and he would not try again.

Then Utgard said: "Will you try something else?" Thor replied that he would. Utgard said: "We have a little game here that the younger children play. The young men think nothing of lifting my cat. I would not propose it to you if you had not failed in drinking."

The cat ran in, and Thor did his best. But he could only lift one paw from the ground.

Then he called for someone to wrestle with him, but Utgard said the men would think it beneath them to wrestle with Thor. Then he called his old nurse, Elle, to wrestle with him.

The tighter Thor gripped the old woman, the firmer she stood. Soon he was thrown on one knee, and Utgard sent the old woman away.

The next morning at dawn, Thor and Loke and the two children prepared to go away.

Utgard gave them breakfast and went a little way with them.

When he was ready to go back, he asked Thor how he liked his visit. Thor replied that he had done himself dishonor.

At this Utgard said: "I will tell you the truth now that we are out of my palace. You shall never come into it again. If I had known your strength, you should not have come this time.

"In the forest, it was me you met. If I had not held a mountain between your hammer and my head, you would have killed me. There is the mountain. The three caves you see were made by the three blows of your hammer.

"One end of the drinking horn stood in the sea. When you come to the shore, you will see how much water is gone.

"What you took for a cat was the great Midgard Serpent which encircles the earth and holds its tail in its mouth. The nurse was old age. No one can resist her."

Hearing this, Thor raised his hammer to strike. But Utgard and the palace vanished and left only a grassy plain.

THOR AND THRYM

When Thor was away on one of his journeys, he laid his hammer down for a moment and went away without it.

The giant Thrym found the hammer. He carried it to Jotunheim and buried it eight miles deep.

When Thor missed his hammer, he went back and found that it was gone. He knew that no one but a giant could have lifted it.

Back he drove to Asgard in such a rage that the gods themselves trembled. But they trembled still more when they heard Thor's story. They feared that the giants could no longer be kept out of Asgard.

Loke borrowed Freya's falcon plumage and flew to Jotunheim. The first giant he met was Thrym. "Why have you come to Jotunheim?" said the giant. "I have come for Thor's hammer," replied Loke. "Ho! Ho! Ho! "Laughed the giant, " the hammer is buried eight miles deep. I will give it to no one until he brings me Freya for a wife."

Loke flew swiftly back to Asgard and told Thor what the giant had said.

Thor thought of nothing but his precious hammer. He rushed to Freya and told her to make ready to go to Jotunheim.

At this, Freya was so angry, that Thor, big as he was, trembled and went out without saying anything more.

Loke said, "We will dress you up like a woman, and what a beautiful bride you will be."

So Thor had Freya's dress put on him, a necklace around his great throat, and a veil over his face. But even then his eyes blazed like fire.

Loke dressed himself as a maid, and they went to Jotunheim in Thor's chariot.

When Thrym saw them coming, he had a great feast prepared.

Thor ate a whole ox and ten salmon. Thrym's eyes stood out with surprise. But Loke whispered, "Freya longed so much to come to Jotunheim that she has eaten nothing for seven days."

At this, Thrym was so pleased that he leaned over to look into her face. But he started back when he saw the blazing eyes.

Loke said softly, "Freya longed so much to come to Jotunheim that she has not slept for seven nights."

When the feast was over, Thrym brought the hammer and laid it in Freya's lap.

The moment Thor's fingers touched the handle he sprang up, tore the veil from his eyes and drew back the hammer to strike.

So angry was he that he laid the giant dead with one blow.

Thor and Loke went away, leaving nothing but a heap of blazing sticks where the house had been.

THOR AND GEIRROD

Once Loke put on Freya's falcon plumage and flew away to Jotunheim. As he flew about amusing himself, he came to the home of the giant Geirrod.

He perched on the roof and looked in through an opening.

Geirrod saw the bird and sent a servant to catch him. The wall was high and slippery. Loke laughed to see how much trouble the servant had to climb up.

He thought he would fly away when the servant had almost reached him. But when he tried to fly away, his feet were fast. So he was caught and taken to Geirrod.

As soon as Geirrod looked into the falcon's eyes, he knew he was not a bird. The giant asked Loke many questions, but Loke would not answer a word.

Geirrod locked him in a chest for three months without food.

At last, Loke confessed who he was. To save his life, he promised to get Thor to go to Geirrod's house without his hammer and belt.

Loke went at once to Thor and told him Geirrod wanted to fight him.

Thor's eyes began to flash fire, and he rushed to his house for his hammer and belt. But Loke had been there before him and hidden them.

Thor was so angry that he would not wait to find them. Away he went in his chariot to fight the giant.

On the way, he met a giantess who told him Geirrod was a dog-wise and dangerous giant.

She gave Thor her gloves and staff and belt of strength.

Soon Thor reached a wide river. He put on his belt of strength and plunged into the water.

When he reached the middle of the river, the waves went over his shoulders.

Thor looked up and saw that Geirrod's daughter was making the waves with her hand. He threw a stone and drove her away.

Then he reached the bank and caught a branch and drew himself out of the water.

When Thor reached Geirrod's house, he was given a room by himself. There was only one chair in the room.

Thor sat in the chair. Suddenly it was lifted to the roof. He raised his staff and pressed against the roof with all his strength.

The chair fell to the floor. Two of Geirrod's daughters had been sitting under it.

Soon Geirrod sent a servant to invite Thor to come and see games.

Great fires burned all down the hall. When Thor came near Geirrod, the giant seized a piece of iron and threw it at Thor.

Thor caught it in his iron gloves and raised his arm to throw it at Geirrod.

Geirrod ran behind a post. Thor hurled the iron. It went through the post and Geirrod, and through the wall into the ground outside.

Thor took the gloves and staff and belt back to the giantess. He never went anywhere without his hammer again.

THE APPLES OF IDUN

One day Odin and Loke were traveling together. They came to a field where a herd of black-horned oxen was grazing. They were very hungry, so they killed one of the oxen. But they tried in vain to cook the meat. It stayed raw in spite of the hottest fire they could make.

A huge eagle flew to a tree near them and said out loud, "I will make the fire burn if you share the meat with me." The gods were very glad to do anything that would give them food. So they promised to share with the eagle.

In a short time, the meat was cooked. The eagle flew down and laid hold of half of it. But it made Loke angry, and he struck the eagle with a pole. To his surprise, the pole stuck fast, and he could not let it go. He was dragged over rocks and bushes until he begged for mercy.

Then the eagle changed into the renowned giant, Thjasse. The giant said he would not let Loke go until he promised to deliver Idun and her apples into his hands.

Half dead with fright, Loke promised. But he did not know how he could keep his promise because Idun kept the apples in a strong box and every day she gave some of them to the gods.

When Loke returned, he told Idun that he had seen much finer apples than hers just outside of Asgard. Idun wished to compare her apples with those Loke had seen. So she took the box and went with him.

As soon as they were outside, Thjasse came in shape of an eagle. He carried Idun and her apples to Jotunheim. Soon the gods found themselves growing old and gray because they had no apples to eat.

When they inquired, they found that Loke was at the bottom of the mischief as usual. The gods threatened to kill Loke if he did not bring back Idun and her apples.

Loke was frightened. He borrowed Freya's falcon plumage and flew to Jotunheim.

Thjasse was out fishing, then Loke changed Idun into a nut and flew back to Asgard with the nut between his claws. Thjasse saw him and followed closely.

The gods feared Loke would be overtaken. So they put chips on the walls of Asgard. The instant Loke was over, they set fire to the chips.

Thjasse could not stop in time, and his eagle plumage was burned. He fell down into the streets of the city and was killed by the gods.

FREY AND GERD

No god was allowed to sit on Odin's throne but Odin himself.

One day when Frey was alone in the palace, he sat upon the throne and looked over into Jotunheim.

There he saw a maiden come out of a low, dark house. As she walked down the pathway, the air became clearer and warmer. The earth brightened and grew green. When she went inside and shut the door, the light faded, and the earth grew black again.

Around the low, dark house, was a wavering wall of fire, and within the wall, fierce dogs kept watch, night and day.

When the door was shut, and Frey could no longer see the maiden, he went away sadly. He could neither eat nor sleep for longing to see her.

So sad was he that no one dared ask him his trouble. Skade, his mother, sent Skirner, his faithful friend, to find out what ailed him.

Frey told Skirner of the beautiful maiden, and that he could never be happy unless she came to Asgard. Then Skirner said if he could have Frey's horse and sword, he would ride through the flame wall, kill the watchdog and bring Gerd to Asgard.

Frey gave his horse gladly. Skirner rode through the fire, although it roared in his ears and blazed far above his head.

When the dogs saw him, they set up a fierce howling. But Skirner quieted them with Frey's sword.

Gerd heard the noise outside and sent a servant to see what it was. The servant said an armed warrior stood at the door.

But Gerd knew he must be a god, or he could not have passed the flame wall. So she bade the servant bring him in and give him food and drink.

As soon as Skirner saw Gerd, he took from his pocket eleven of the golden apples of the gods and offered them to her as a present from Frey. But Gerd would not have the apples. Then Skirner offered her the wonderful golden ring made by Sindre. This, also, she refused.

Then Skirner took out a magic wand and waved it over the maiden. As he waved the wand, he sang a magic song, telling of the warmth and light of Asgard and the beauty and gentleness of Frey.

As the maiden listened, she became enchanted with the glory of the city of the gods, and no longer remembered her own cheerless land. Then Skirner took her behind him on Frey's horse and rode back across the rainbow bridge.

Frey stood by the gate watching, and when he found that Skirner had not only brought Gerd but that he had made her forget her home and love Asgard, he was so pleased that he let Skirner keep his sword.

GODS OF OLYMPUS

ZEUS

In the northern part of Greece there was a very high mountain called Mount Olympus; so high that during almost all the year its top was covered with snow, and often, too, it was wrapped in clouds. Its sides were very steep, and covered with thick forests of oak and beech trees.

The Greeks thought that the palaces of their gods were above the top of this mountain, far out of the reach of men, and hidden from their sight by the clouds. Here they thought that the gods met together in a grand council hall, and held great feasts, at which they talked over the affairs of the whole world.

Zeus, who ruled over the land and the air, was the king of the gods and was the greatest and strongest among them. The strength of all the other gods put together could not overcome him. It was he who caused the clouds to form, and who sent the rain to refresh the thirsty earth. His great weapon was the thunderbolt, which he carried in his right hand. But the thunderbolt was seldom used because the frown and angry nod of Zeus were enough to shake the palaces of the gods themselves.

Although Zeus was so powerful, he was also kind and generous to those who pleased him. The people who lived upon the earth loved as well as feared him and called him father. He was the most just of all the gods. Once when there was a great war between the Greeks and another people, all the other gods took sides and tried to help those whom they favored all they could. But Zeus did not. He tried to be just, and at last, he gave the victory to the side which he thought deserved to have it.

The oak was thought to be sacred to Zeus because it was the strongest and grandest of all the trees. In one part of Greece, there was a forest of these, which was called the forest of Dodona. It was so thick and that the sunbeams scarcely found their way through the leaves to the moss upon the ground. Here the wind made strange low sounds among the knotted branches, and people soon began to think that this was their great god Zeus speaking to men through the leaves of his favorite tree. So they set this forest apart as sacred to him; and only his servants, who were called priests, were allowed to live in it. People came to this place from all parts of Greece to ask the advice of the god, and the priests would consult with him, and hear his answers in the murmuring of the wind among the branches.

The Greeks also built beautiful temples for their gods, as we build churches. To these temples they brought rich gifts of gold and silver and other precious things, to show how thankful they were for the help which the gods gave them. In each temple, there was a great block of marble called the altar, and on this, a small fire was often kept burning by the priests. If anyone wished to get the help of one of the gods, he would bring a dove, or a goat, or an ox to the temple, so that the priests might kill it, and burn part of its flesh as an offering. They thought that the smell of the burning flesh pleased the gods.

Since Zeus was the greatest of the gods, many of the most beautiful temples in Greece were built in his honor. A part of one of these temples to Zeus is still standing, and you can see it if you ever go to Greece. It was made of the finest white marble and was surrounded on all sides by rows of tall columns beautifully carved.

In another temple, there was a great statue of Zeus, made of ivory and gold. It was over sixty feet high and showed the god seated on a great throne which was covered with carving. The robe of the god was of solid gold. But it was the face of the statue which the Greeks thought was most wonderful. It was so grand and beautiful that they said: "Either the sculptor must have gone up to heaven and seen Zeus upon his throne, or the god must have come down to earth and shown his face to the artist."

Besides building temples for their gods, the Greeks held great festivals in their honor also. The greatest of these festivals was the one which was held in honor of Zeus at a place called Olympia. Every four years messengers would go about from town to town to give notice of it. Then all wars would cease, and people from all over Greece would come to Olympia to worship the god. There they would find the swiftest runners racing for a wreath of olive leaves as a prize. There they would also find chariot races and wrestling matches and other games. The Greeks believed that Zeus and the other gods loved to see men using their strength and skill to do them honor at their festivals. So for months and months beforehand, men practiced for these games; and the one who gained the victory, in them was looked upon as ever after the favorite of gods and men.

I will sing of Zeus, chiefest among the gods and greatest, all-seeing, the lord of all, the fulfiller who whispers words of wisdom to Themis as she sits leaning towards him.

Be gracious, all-seeing Son of Cronos, most excellent and great!

Homeric Hymn 23, To the Son of Cronos

POSEIDON

Poseidon was the brother of Zeus, and just as Zeus ruled over the land and the sky, Poseidon ruled over the rivers and the seas. He was always represented as carrying a trident, or fish spear with three points. When he struck the sea with this, fierce storms would arise; then with a word, he could quiet the dashing waves, and make the surface of the water as smooth as that of a pond.

The palace of Poseidon was said to be at the bottom of the sea. It was made of shells and coral, fastened together with gold and silver. The floors were of pearl and were ornamented with all kinds of precious stones. Around the palace were great gardens filled with beautiful sea plants and vines. The flowers were of the softest and most delicate tints and were far more beautiful than those growing in the light of the sun. The leaves were not of the deep green which we see on land, but of a most lovely sea green color. If you should ever go to the sea coast, and look down through the water, perhaps you also might see the gardens of Poseidon lying among the rocks at the bottom of the sea.

Poseidon rode over the surface of the sea in a chariot made of a huge sea shell, which was drawn by great sea horses with golden hoofs and manes. At the approach of the god, the waves would grow quiet, and strange fishes and huge sea serpents and sea lions would come to the surface to play about his chariot. Wonderful creatures called Tritons went before and beside his chariot, blowing upon shells as trumpets. These Tritons had green hair and eyes; their bodies were like those of men, but instead of legs they had tails like fishes.

Nymphs also swam along by the sea god's chariot. Some of these were like the Tritons, half human and half fish. Others were like lovely maidens, with fair faces and hair. Some lived so much in the depths of the sea that their soft blue eyes could not bear the light of day. So they never left the water except in the evening, when they would find some quiet place upon the shore, and dance to the music which they made upon delicate sea shells.

Poseidon once had a quarrel with one of the goddesses over a piece of land which each one wished to own, and at last, they asked the other gods to settle the dispute for them. So at a meeting on Mount Olympus, the gods decided that the one who should make the most useful gift to the people should have the land.

When the trial came, Poseidon thought that a spring of water would be an excellent gift. He struck a great blow with his trident upon a rocky hill that stood in that land, and a stream of water gushed forth. But Poseidon had lived so much in the sea that he had forgotten that men could drink only fresh water. The spring which he had made was as salt as salt could be, and it was of no use to the people at all. Then the goddess, in her turn, caused an olive tree to spring up out of the ground. When the gods saw how much use men could make of its fruit and oil, they decided that the goddess had won. So Poseidon did not get the land, but ever afterward the people showed the salt spring and the olive tree upon the hilltop as a proof that the trial had taken place.

Poseidon was worshiped most by the people who lived by the shore of the sea. Every city along the coast had a temple to Poseidon, where people came to pray to him for fair weather and happy voyages for themselves and their friends.

I begin to sing about Poseidon, the great god, the mover of the earth and fruitless sea, god of the deep who is also lord of Helicon and wide Aegae. A two-fold office the gods allotted you, O Shaker of the Earth, to be a tamer of horses and a savior of ships!

Hail, Poseidon, Holder of the Earth, dark-haired lord! O blessed one, be kindly in heart and help those who voyage in ships!

Homeric Hymn 22, To Poseidon

HADES

Hades, the god of the underworld, was also a brother of Zeus; but the Greeks did not think of him as being bright and beautiful like the other gods. They believed, indeed, that he helped make the seeds sprout and push their leaves above the surface of the earth, and that he gave men the gold and silver which they dug out of their mines. But more often they thought of him as the god of the gloomy world of the dead; so they imagined that he was dark and stern in appearance, and they feared him more than they did the other gods.

The Greeks thought that when anyone died, his soul or shade went at once to the kingdom of Hades. The way to this underworld lay through a cave which was in the midst of a dark and gloomy forest, by the side of a still lake. When they had passed down through this cavern, the shades came to a broad, swift stream of black water. There they found a bent old man named Charon, whose duty it was to take the shades across the stream in a small, leaky boat. But only those spirits whose bodies had been properly burned or buried in the world above could cross; and those whose funerals had not been properly attended to, were compelled to wander for a hundred years upon the river bank before Charon would take them across.

When the shades had crossed the river, they came upon a terrible creature, which guarded the path so that no one who had once passed into the kingdom of the dead could ever come out again. This was the great dog Cerberus, who had three heads, and who barked so fiercely that he could be heard through all the lower world.

Beyond him, the shades entered the judgment room, where they were judged for what they had done on earth. If they had lived good lives, they were allowed to enter the fields of the blessed, where flowers of gold bloomed in beautiful meadows; and there they walked and talked with other shades, who had led good lives in the world above. But the Greeks thought that even these spirits were always longing to see the light of day again because they believed that no life was as happy as that which they lived on the face of the earth.

The shades who had lived bad lives in the world above were dreadfully punished in the world of the dead. There was once a king named Sisyphus, who had been cruel and wicked all his life. When he died, and his shade went down to the underworld, the judge told him that his punishment would be to roll a great stone up a steep hill and down the other side. At first, Sisyphus thought that this would be an easy thing to do. But when he had got the stone almost to the top, and it seemed that one more push would send it over and end his task, it suddenly slipped from his hands and rolled to the foot of the hill again. So it happened every time, and the Greeks believed that Sisyphus would have to keep working in this way as long as the world lasted and that his task would never be done.

There was once another king, named Tantalus, who was wealthy and fortunate upon earth and had been loved by the gods of heaven. Zeus had even invited him to sit at his table once and had told him the secrets of the gods. But Tantalus had not proved worthy of all this honor. He had not been able to keep the secrets that had been trusted to him but had told them to all the world. So when his shade came before the judge of the dead, he, too, was given a dreadful punishment. He was chained in the midst of a sparkling little lake where the water came up almost to his lips. He was always burning with thirst; but whenever he stooped to drink from the lake, the water sank into the ground before him. He was always hungry, and branches loaded with delicious fruits hung just over him. But whenever he raised his hand to gather them, the breeze swung them just out of his reach. In this way, the Greeks thought that Tantalus was to be punished forever because he had told the secrets of the gods.

HERA

The wife of Zeus was the tall and beautiful goddess Hera. As Zeus was the king of all the gods, so she was their queen. She sat beside him in the council hall of the gods, on a throne only a little less splendid than his own. She was the greatest of all the goddesses and was extremely proud of her own strength and beauty.

Hera chose the peacock for her favorite bird because its plumage was beautiful. The goddess Iris was her servant and messenger and flew swiftly through the air upon her errands. The rainbow, which seemed to join heaven and earth with its beautiful arch, was thought to be the road by which Iris traveled.

Hera was not only proud of her own beauty, but she was also very jealous of the beauty of anyone else. She would even punish women that she thought were too beautiful as if they had done something very wrong; she often did this by changing them into animals or birds. There was one woman whom Hera changed into the form of a savage bear and turned out to wander in the forest because she hated her beautiful face. The poor creature was terribly frightened among the fierce animals of the woods because although she herself now had the form of a beast, her soul was still human. At last Zeus, who was kinder of heart than Hera, took pity upon her. He lifted her far above the earth, and placed her among the stars of heaven; and so, ever after that, the Greeks called one group of stars the Great Bear.

There was once a wood nymph named Echo, who deceived Hera and so made her very angry. Echo was a merry, beautiful girl, whose tongue was always going, and who was never satisfied unless she could have the last word. As a punishment for her deception, Hera took away her voice, leaving her only the power to repeat the last word that should be spoken to her. Echo now no longer cared to join her companions in their merry games, and so wandered through the forests all alone. But she longed to talk, and would often hide in the woods, and repeat the words of hunters and others who passed that way.

At last, she learned to take delight in puzzling and mocking the people who listened to her.

"Who are you?" they would shout at her.
"You," would come her answer.
"Then, who am I?" they would ask, still more puzzled.
"I," Echo would answer in her sweet, teasing manner.

One day Echo met in the woods a young man named Narcissus and loved him. But he was very unkind and would take no notice of her except to tease her for the loss of her voice. She became very unhappy and began to waste away from grief until at last there was nothing left of her but her beautiful mocking voice.

When the gods found what had happened to the lovely Echo they were very angry. To punish Narcissus for his unkindness, they changed him from a strong young man to a weak, delicate flower, which is now always called by his name.

> I sing of golden-throned Hera whom Rhea bare. Queen of the immortals is she, surpassing all in beauty: she is the sister and the wife of loud-thundering Zeus, —the glorious one whom all the blessed throughout high Olympus reverence and honor even as Zeus who delights in thunder.
>
> *Homeric Hymn 12, To Hera*

APOLLO

Apollo was the son of Zeus and was one of the greatest of the gods of Mount Olympus. He was often called the sun god because the Greeks thought that he brought the sun's light and warmth to men. As these are so necessary to every living thing, they thought that Apollo was also the god of health and manly beauty. So he was always represented by the Greeks in their pictures and statues as a strong and beautiful young man.

Apollo was very fond of music, and was in the habit of playing upon the lyre at the feasts of the gods, to the great delight of all who heard him. He was very proud of his skill, and would often have contests with the other gods, and sometimes even with men.

At one of these contests, King Midas was present. But instead of deciding, as was usual, that Apollo was much the more skillful player, he was better pleased with another. Apollo became very angry at this, and to show his opinion of Midas, he changed his ears into those of a donkey.

It was then the turn of Midas to be vexed. He wore a cap which hid his large, ugly ears; and he allowed no one to learn what had happened to him except the man who cut his hair. Midas made this man promise that he would tell no one of his misfortune. But the man longed so to tell that, at last, he could stand it no longer. He went to the edge of a stream, dug a hole in the earth, and whispered into it the secret. Then he filled up the hole and went away satisfied. But up from that spot sprang a bunch of reeds, which immediately began to whisper on every breeze, "King Midas has donkey's ears; King Midas has donkey's ears." And so the story was soon known to the whole world.

The Greeks thought that Apollo caused sudden death among men by shooting swift arrows which never failed of their aim. In this way, he punished the wicked and gave welcome death to the good who were suffering and wished to die.

There was once a great queen named Niobe, who had six sons and six daughters. She was proud of her beauty and proud of her wealth and power, but proudest of all of her twelve beautiful children. She thought that they were so beautiful, and she loved them so much, that she even dared to boast that she was greater than the mother of Apollo, who had but two children.

This made the goddess very angry, and she begged her son to punish the queen for her wicked pride. Apollo, with his bow and arrows at his side, floated down to the earth hid in a cloud. There he saw the sons of Niobe playing games among the other boys of the city. Quickly he pierced one after another of them with his arrows, and soon the six lay dead upon the ground. The frightened people took up the dead boys gently and carried them home to their mother. She was broken hearted, but cried, -"The gods have indeed punished me, but they have left me, my beautiful daughters."

She had scarcely spoken when one after another her daughters fell dead at her feet. Niobe clasped the youngest in her arms to save her from the deadly arrows. When this one, too, was killed, the queen could bear no more. Her great grief turned her to stone, and the people thought that for many years her stone figure stood there with tears constantly flowing from its sad eyes.

One of the most famous temples in Greece was built to Apollo at a place called Delphi. There was always a priestess, whose duty it was to tell the people who came there the answers which the god gave to their questions. She would place herself on a seat over a crack in the earth out of which arose a thin stream of gasses. By breathing this she was made light headed for the moment, and then she was supposed to be able to tell the answer which Apollo gave.

These answers were almost always in poetry; and though they were very wise sayings, it was sometimes hard to tell just what the god meant by them. Once a great king wished to begin a war and asked the advice of Apollo about it at Delphi. The priestess answered, that if he went to war, he would destroy a great nation. The king thought that this must mean that he would conquer his enemies, and so he began the war. But, alas, he was conquered himself and found that it was his own nation which was to be destroyed.

Although these oracles, as they were called, were so hard to understand, the Greeks thought a great deal of them; and they would never begin anything important without first asking the advice of Apollo.

Phoebus, of you even the swan sings with clear voice to the beating of his wings, as he alights upon the bank by the eddying river Peneus; and of you, the sweet-tongued minstrel, holding his high-pitched lyre, always sings both first and last.

And so hail to you, lord! I seek your favor with my song.

Homeric Hymn 21, To Apollo

ATHENA

Athena was one of the most powerful of the goddesses. She was called the daughter of Zeus; but the Greeks believed that she had sprung full-grown from his head, wearing her helmet and armor. She was more warlike than the other goddesses and was almost always successful in her battles.

Athena was the goddess of wisdom and learning. The owl was her favorite bird, because of its wise and solemn look, and it is often represented with Athena in the images which the Greeks made of her.

While Artemis loved most the woods and mountains, Athena liked the cities better. There she watched over the work and occupations of men and helped them to find out better ways of doing things. For them, she invented the plow and the rake, and she taught men to yoke oxen to the plow that they might till the soil better and more easily. She also made the first bridle, and showed men how to tame horses with it, and make them work for them. She invented the chariot, and the flute, and the trumpet, and she taught men how to count and use numbers. Besides all this, Athena was the goddess of spinning and weaving; and she herself could weave the most beautiful cloths of many colors and of the most marvelous patterns.

There was once a girl named Arachne, who was a skillful weaver, and who was also very proud of her skill. Indeed, she was so proud that once she boasted that she could weave as well as the goddess Athena herself. The goddess heard this boast and came to Arachne in the form of an old woman. She advised the girl to take back her words, but Arachne refused. Then the bent old woman changed suddenly into the goddess Athena. Arachne was startled and surprised, but in an instant, she was ready for the test of skill which the goddess demanded. The two stood at looms side by side and wove cloth covered with the most wonderful pictures. When the goddess discovered that she could find no fault with Arachne's work, she became terribly angry. She struck Arachne and tore the cloth on her loom. Arachne was so frightened by the anger of the goddess that she tried to kill herself. Athena then became sorry for the girl and saved her life by changing her into a spider. So Arachne lives to this day, and still weaves the most wonderful of all webs upon our walls and ceilings, and upon the grasses by the roadside.

It was not often, though, that Athena was so spiteful as you must think her from the story of Arachne. Usually, she was kind and generous; and nothing pleased her better than to help brave, honest men, especially if they were skillful and clever.

The Greeks loved to tell the story of one such man whom Athena helped. His name was Odysseus, and in a great war of the Greeks, he had proved himself to be one of the bravest and most cunning of all their chiefs. But in some way, he had displeased the god Poseidon so much that when the war was over, and all the other Greeks sailed away in safety, Poseidon would not permit him to reach his far-off home. So for ten years, Odysseus was kept far from his wife and child. He was blown about by storms, his ship was wrecked, and he had to meet and overcome giants and all sorts of monsters. Indeed, he had to make a trip down into the dark world of the dead before he could find out how he might manage to get back to his home again. But through it all, Athena was his friend. She watched over him and encouraged him, and in each difficulty, she taught him some trick by which he could escape. At last, after he had suffered much, and had even lost all of the men who had started with him, she brought him safely home again, in spite of all that Poseidon could do to prevent it.

> Of Pallas Athene, guardian of the city, I begin to sing. Dread is she, and with Ares, she loves deeds of war, the sack of cities and the shouting and the

battle. It is she who saves the people as they go out to war and come back.

Hail, goddess, and give us good fortune with happiness!

Homeric Hymn 11, To Athena

APHRODITE

The most beautiful of all the goddesses was Aphrodite, the goddess of love and beauty. She was often called the "sea-born" goddess because she was formed one evening from the foam of the sea, where its waves beat upon a rocky shore. Her eyes were as blue as the summer sky overhead, her skin as fair as the white sea foam from which she came, and her hair as golden as the yellow rays of the setting sun. When she stepped from the water upon the beach, flowers sprang up under her feet; and when she was led into the assembly of the gods, everyone admired and loved her.

Zeus, in order to make up for his cruelty to Hephaestus, he gave him this beautiful goddess for his wife. The gods prepared for them the grandest wedding possible. All the gods and goddesses were there, bringing with them magnificent gifts for the bride. But the most wonderful of all were the presents given her by Hephaestus himself.

He built many palaces for her, the most marvelous of which was on the island of Cyprus. In the middle of this island was a large blue lake, in which there was another island. Upon this, Hephaestus built a palace of white marble, with towers and ornaments of gold and silver. It was then filled with wonderful things which the skillful god made to please his wife. Among these were servants of solid gold that would obey the wishes of Aphrodite without word or sound. There were also golden harps, which made sweet music all day long, without anyone playing upon them; and golden birds, which sang the sweetest of songs.

All birds were great favorites of Aphrodite, and they loved her as much as she loved them. They taught her their bird language so that she talked with them as though they had been persons. Of all them, however, she liked the doves and swans the best. Doves fluttered around her head and alighted, on her arms and shoulders, wherever she went; and swans drew her back and forth in a beautiful boat across the waters between her palace and the shore of the lake.

Aphrodite was the kindest and gentlest of the goddesses. The Greeks did not pray to her for power, as they did to Zeus, or for learning and wisdom, as they did to Athena. Instead, they prayed to her to make the persons they cared for love them in return

Once a sculptor, named Pygmalion, tried to make a statue that should be more lovely than the loveliest woman. He chose the finest ivory, and for months and months, he worked patiently at his task. As it began to take the form of a beautiful maiden under his skillful chisel, he became so interested in his work that he scarcely took time to eat or sleep. At last, the work was finished, and everybody said that the statue was more beautiful than any woman that had ever lived.

But Pygmalion was not satisfied. All day long he would sit in front of his statue and look at it. He came to love it so much that he wished over and over again that it were a real woman so that it might talk to him, and love him in return. He longed for this in secret until at last, he grew bold enough to ask the gods for help. Then he went to the temple of Aphrodite, and there before the altar he prayed to the goddess to change his statue into a real woman. As he finished his prayer, he saw the altar fire flame up three times, and he knew that the goddess had heard him. He hastened home, and there he found that his statue of ivory had indeed been turned into a woman of flesh and blood; and all his life long, he blessed the goddess Aphrodite for granting his wish.

> Of Cythera, born in Cyprus, I will sing. She gives kindly gifts to men: smiles are ever on her lovely face, and lovely is the brightness that plays over it.

> Hail, goddess, queen of well-built Salamis and sea-girt Cyprus; grant me a cheerful song. And now I will remember you and another song also.
>
> *Homeric Hymn 10, To Apphrodite*

HERMES

The Greeks did not always think of their gods as grown up persons. Sometimes they told stories of their youth and even of their babyhood. According to these stories the god Hermes, who was the son of Zeus, must have been a very wonderful child. They said that when he was but a day old, his nurses left him asleep, as they supposed, in his cradle. But the moment that their backs were turned, he climbed out and ran away.

For quite a while he wandered about over the fields and hills, until, by and by, he came upon a herd of cattle that belonged to his elder brother Apollo. These he drove off and hid in a cave in the mountains. Then, as he thought that by this time his nurses would be expecting him to wake up, he started for home. On the way, he came upon a tortoise shell in the road, and from this, he made a harp or lyre by stretching strings tightly across it. He amused himself by playing upon this until he reached home, where he crept back into his cradle again.

Apollo soon discovered the loss of his fine cattle and was told by an old man that the baby Hermes had driven them away. He went to the mother of Hermes in great anger and told her that her baby had stolen his cattle. She was astonished, of course, that anyone should say such a thing of a baby only a day old, and showed Apollo the child lying in his cradle, fast asleep as it seemed. But Apollo was not deceived by the child's innocent look. He insisted upon taking him to Mount Olympus; and there before his father Zeus, and the other gods, he accused Hermes of having stolen the herd of oxen.

At first, Hermes denied that he had done anything of the kind; and he talked so fast and so well, in defending himself, that all the gods were amused and delighted. Zeus, however, was the most pleased of all because he was proud of a son who could do such wonderful things while he was so young. But for all his cleverness, Hermes, at last, had to confess that he had driven the cattle off, and had to go with Apollo, and show him where he had hidden them.

All this time Hermes had with him the lyre which he had made from the tortoise shell, and as they went along, he began to play upon this for Apollo. As you know, Apollo was very fond of music, so he was greatly delighted with this new instrument which Hermes had invented. When Hermes saw how pleased Apollo was, he gave him the lyre. Apollo was so charmed with the gift, that he quite forgave Hermes for the trick he played him, and, indeed, gave him the whole herd of cattle for his own, in return for the little lyre.

As soon as he was grown, Hermes was made the messenger, or herald, of the gods. He was chosen for this position because he had shown so early that he was a good talker, and so would be able to deliver the messages well. In order that he might be able to do his errands quickly, he wore a pair of winged sandals on his feet, which carried him through the air as swiftly as a flash of lightning.

He was especially the herald of Zeus. The Greeks thought that their dreams came from Zeus himself, and that is was Hermes who brought them, flying swiftly downward through the darkness of the night. But besides this, Hermes served as a messenger for all the gods, even for Hades in the underworld. When people died, the Greeks thought that it was Hermes who guided their shades to their dark home underneath the ground

Because he traveled so much himself, Hermes was supposed to take care of all men who traveled upon the earth. In those days it was a far more dangerous thing to make a journey than it is now. Then men had to walk nearly always when they wished to go from one place to another. The roads were bad and often were only narrow paths that one could scarcely follow. In some places, too, there were robbers who would lie in wait for travelers coming along that way. So, before starting, travelers would offer sacrifices to Hermes, and pray to him to protect them, and grant them a safe journey. All along the roads, were posts of wood, upon which the head of Hermes was carved. These usually stood at the meeting of two roads and were guideposts, to tell the travelers which way to take.

I sing of Cyllenian Hermes, the Slayer of Argus, lord of Cyllene and Arcadia rich in flocks, luck-bringing messenger of the deathless gods. He was born of Maia, the daughter of Atlas, when she had made with Zeus, -- a shy goddess she. Ever she avoided the throng of the blessed gods and lived in a shadowy cave, and there the Son of Cronos used to lie with the rich-tressed nymph at dead of night,

while white-armed Hera lay bound in sweet sleep:
and neither deathless god nor mortal man knew it.

And so hail to you, Son of Zeus and Maia; with you,
I have begun: now I will turn to another song! Hail,
Hermes, giver of grace, guide, and giver of good
things!

Homeric Hymn 18, To Hermes

HESTIA

Hestia had fewer temples than any of the other
gods of Mount Olympus, but she was worshiped the most
of all. This was because she was the hearth goddess, that
is, the goddess of the fireside, and so had part in all the
worship of the Greek home.

The Greeks said that it was Hestia who first taught
men how to build houses. As their houses were so very
different from the ones in which we live, perhaps you
would like to know something about them. In the days
when these old Greeks were so brave and noble and had
such beautiful thoughts about the world, they did not care
much what kind of houses they lived in. The weather in
their country was so fine that they did not stay indoors
very much. Besides, they cared more about building
suitable temples for the gods and putting up beautiful

statues about the city, than they did about building fine houses for themselves.

So their houses were usually very small and plain. They did not have a yard around the houses, but built them close together, as we do in some of our large cities. Instead of having their yard in front, or at the sides of the house, they had it in the middle, with the house built all around it. That is the way many people in other lands build their houses even now, and this inner yard they call a courtyard. Around three sides of the courtyard, the Greeks had pleasant porches in which the boys and girls could play when it was too hot for them to be out in the open yard. And opening off on all sides from the porches were the rooms of the house.

In the middle of one of the largest of these rooms, there was always an altar to the goddess Hestia. This was a block of stone on which a fire was always kept burning. The Greeks did not have chimneys to their houses, so they would leave a square hole in the roof just over the altar to let the smoke out. And as they had no stoves, all the food for the family was usually cooked over this fire on the altar.

Whenever there was any change made in the family, they offered sacrifices to Hestia. If a baby was born, or if there was a wedding, or if one of the family died, they must sacrifice to Hestia. Also whenever anyone set out on a journey, or returned home from one, and even when a new slave was brought into the family, Hestia must be worshiped, or else they were afraid some evil would come upon their home.

The Greeks thought that the people of a city were just a larger family, so they thought that every city, as well as every house, must have an altar to Hestia. In the town hall, where the men who ruled the city met together, there was an altar to the goddess of the hearth; and on it, too, a fire was always kept burning. These old Greeks were very careful never to let this altar fire go out. If by any chance it did go out, then they were not allowed to start it again from another fire, or even to kindle it by striking a bit of flint and piece of steel together, because of course, they had not matches. They were obliged to kindle it either by rubbing two dry sticks together, or else by means of a burning glass. Otherwise, they thought Hestia would be displeased.

The Greeks were a daring people, and very fond of going to sea, and trading with distant countries. Sometimes, indeed, part of the people of a city would decide to leave their old home, and start a new city in some far-off place with which they traded. When such a party started out, they always carried with them some of the sacred fire from the altar of Hestia in the mother city. With this, they would light the altar fire in their new home. In this way, the worship of Hestia helped to make the Greeks feel that they were all members of one great family, and prevented those who went away from forgetting the city from which they came.

> Hestia, you who tend the holy house of the lord Apollo, the Far-shooter at goodly Pytho, with soft oil dripping ever from your locks, come now into this house, come, having one mind with Zeus the all-wise -- draw near, and withal bestow grace upon my song.
>
> *Homeric Hymn 24, To Hestia*

DIONYSUS

The gods of Mount Olympus did not always remain high up in heaven, out of the reach and sight of men. The Greeks told many stories of what they did on earth as well. Artemis loved to wander over the mountains and hunt the deer in the forests. Hephaestus had his workshops wherever there were great volcanoes. Hermes often appeared to men as a messenger from Zeus, and the other gods also would often come down in the shape of men or women to give advice or reproof to their favorites.

But the god Dionysus did much more than this. For many years he lived on earth among men. He was the son of Zeus, though he was brought up on earth by forest spirits. Perhaps it was from these that he learned to love fresh growing plants and climbing vines full of fruit; but however that may be, he became the god of the grape and wine. When he was grown, he did not join the other gods on Mount Olympus but set out on a long, long journey through all the countries of the world, teaching men everywhere how to plant and tend the grapevine, and how to press the juice from the ripe fruit, and make it into wine.

With him, in his journeys, went bands of strange wood spirits, who danced and made music before him, and waited upon him. Wherever he and his band were well treated, the god was kind and generous to all and taught many useful things. But sometimes the kings did not want their people to learn the new things which he taught, and then he would punish the selfish rulers very severely.

At one time during his journey, Dionysus was wandering alone on a sea beach, when a ship came sailing by near the shore. The men in the ship were pirates; and as soon as they saw the beautiful youth, they sent men ashore, who seized him, and carried him aboard the ship. They expected to sell him as a slave in some distant country because in those days anyone who happened to be made a prisoner could be sold into slavery. But the pirates soon discovered that their prisoner was not an ordinary person. When they tried to tie him so that he could not escape, the ropes fell off his hands and feet of their own accord. Then suddenly the masts and sails became covered with climbing vines full of bunches of rich, ripe grapes, and streams of bubbling wine flowed through the ship. This was all very astonishing to the pirates; and when the prisoner changed from a slender young man into a roaring lion and sprang upon their captain, they became very much frightened. When a great bear also appeared in their midst, they could stand it no longer, and all jumped overboard except one who had wanted to set the prisoner free. As he, too, was about to jump, Dionysus changed back into his own form and told him to stay and have no fear. The god even took pity on the others and saved them from drowning by changing them into dolphins.

When Dionysus had finished his long journey, he went up to Mount Olympus and took his place among the other gods. The people of the earth worshiped him in temples, as they did the other gods; but besides this, they held great festivals in his honor each year. One of these festivals came in the springtime when the vines began to grow; and another when the grapes had ripened, and the wine had been made. At these festivals, the people had great processions, and men would go about singing and dancing as the wood spirits had sung and danced before Dionysus on his journey. Poets, too, would sing verses to the music of the lyre, and in these, they told about the adventures of the god. At length, they began to have theaters, and regular performances in them, at these festivals. So Dionysus became not only the god of the grape and wine but also of the theater.

> I begin to sing of ivy-crowned Dionysus, the loud-crying god, splendid son of Zeus and glorious Semele. The rich-haired Nymphs received him in their bosoms from the lord his father and fostered and nurtured him carefully in the dells of Nysa, where by the will of his father he grew up in a sweet-smelling cave, being reckoned among the immortals. But when the goddesses had brought him up, a god oft hymned, then began he to wander continually through the woody coombes, thickly wreathed with ivy and laurel. And the Nymphs followed in his train with him for their leader, and the boundless forest was filled with their outcry.

And so hail to you, Dionysus, god of abundant clusters! Grant that we may come again rejoicing to this season, and from that season onwards for many a year.

Homeric Hymn 26, To Dionysus

LEGENDS OF EGYPT

THE DESTRUCTION OF MANKIND

The text containing the Legend of the Destruction of Mankind is written in hieroglyphs and is found on the four walls of a small chamber which is entered from the "hall of columns" in the tomb of Seti I., which is situated on the west bank of the Nile at Thebes. On the wall facing the door of this chamber is painted in red the figure of the large "Cow of Heaven." The lower part of her belly is decorated with a series of thirteen stars, and immediately beneath it are the two Boats of Ra, called Semketet and Mantchet, or Sektet and Matet. Each of her four legs is held in position by two gods, and the god Shu, with outstretched uplifted arms, supports her body.

The legend takes us back to the time when the gods of Egypt went about in the country, and mingled with men and were thoroughly acquainted with their desires and needs. The king who reigned over Egypt was Ra, the Sun god, who was not, however, the first of the Dynasty of Gods who ruled the land. His predecessor on the throne was Hephaistos, who, according to Manetho, reigned 9000 years, while Ra reigned only 992 years; Panodorus makes his reign to have lasted less than 100 years. It seems that the "self-created and self-begotten" god Ra had been ruling over mankind for a very long time, because his subjects were murmuring against him, and they were complaining that he was old, that his bones were like silver, his body like gold, and his hair like lapis-lazuli. When Ra heard these murmurings, he ordered his bodyguard to summon all the gods who had been with him in the Primeval World Ocean, and to bid them privately to assemble in the Great House, which can be no other than the famous temple of Heliopolis. This statement is interesting because it proves that the legend is of Heliopolitan origin, like the cult of Ra itself, and that it does not belong, at least in so far as it applies to Ra, to the Predynastic Period.

When Ra entered the Great Temple, the gods made obeisance to him, and took up their positions on each side of him, and informed him that they awaited his words. Addressing Nu, the personification of the World Ocean,

Ra bade them take notice of the fact that the men and women whom his Eye had created were murmuring against him. He then asked them to consider the matter and to devise a plan of action for him because he was unwilling to slay the rebels without hearing what his gods had to say. In reply, the gods advised Ra to send forth his Eye to destroy the blasphemers since there was no eye on earth that could resist it, especially when it took the form of the goddess Hathor. Ra accepted their advice and sent forth his Eye in the form of Hathor to destroy them, and, though the rebels had fled to the mountains in fear, the Eye pursued, overtook and destroyed them. Hathor rejoiced in her work of destruction, and on her return was praised by Ra, for what she had done. The slaughter of men began at Suten-henen (Herakleopolis), and during the night Hathor waded about in the blood of men. Ra asserted his intention of being master of the rebels, and this is probably referred to in the Book of the Dead, Chapter XVII., in which it is said that Ra rose as king for the first time in Suten- henen. Osiris also was crowned at Suten-henen, and in this city lived the great Bennu bird or Phoenix, and the "Crusher of Bones" mentioned in the Negative Confession.

The legend now goes on to describe an act of Ra, the significance of which it is difficult to explain. The god ordered messengers to be brought to him, and when they arrived, he commanded them to run like the wind to Abu, or the city of Elephantine, and to bring him large quantities of the fruit called Tataat. What kind of fruit this was is not clear, but Brugsch thought they were "mandrakes," the so-called "love-apples," and this translation of Tataat may be used provisionally. The mandrakes were given to Sekti, a goddess of Heliopolis, to crush and grind up, and when this was done, they were mixed with human blood and put in a large brewing of beer which the women slaves had made from wheat. In all, they made 7,000 vessels of beer. When Ra saw the beer, he approved of it and ordered it to be carried up the river to where the goddess Hathor was still engaged in slaughtering men. During the night, he caused this beer to be poured out into the meadows of the Four Heavens, and when Hathor came, she saw the beer with human blood and mandrakes in it, and drank of it and became drunk, and paid no further attention to men and women. In welcoming the goddess, Ra called her "Amit," i.e., "beautiful one," and from this time onward "beautiful women were found in the city of Amit," which was situated in the Western Delta, near Lake Mareotis. Ra also ordered that in future at every one of his festivals vessels of "sleep-producing beer" should be made and that their number should be the same as the number of the handmaidens of Ra. Those who took part in these festivals of Hathor and Ra drank beer in very large quantities, and under the influence of the "beautiful women," i.e., the priestesses, who were supposed to resemble Hathor in their physical attractions, the festal celebrations degenerated into drunken and licentious orgies.

Soon after this, Ra complained that he was smitten with pain and that he was weary of the children of men. He thought them a worthless remnant and wished that more of them had been slain. The gods about him begged him to endure and reminded him that his power was in proportion to his will. Ra was, however, unconsoled, and he complained that his limbs were weak for the first time in his life. Thereupon the god Nu told Shu to help Ra, and he ordered Nut to take the great god Ra on her back. Nut changed herself into a cow, and with the help of Shu, Ra got on her back. As soon as men saw that Ra was on the back of the Cow of Heaven, and was about to leave them, they became filled with fear and repentance and cried out to Ra to remain with them and to slay all those who had blasphemed against him. But the Cow moved on her way and carried Ra to Het-Ahet, a town of the nome of Mareotis, where in later days the right leg of Osiris was said to be preserved. Meanwhile, darkness covered the land. When day broke, the men who had repented of their blasphemies appeared with their bows, and slew the enemies of Ra. At this result, Ra was pleased, and he forgave those who had repented because of their righteous slaughter of his enemies. From this time onwards, human sacrifices were offered up at the festivals of Ra celebrated in this place, and at Heliopolis and in other parts of Egypt.

After these things, Ra declared to Nut that he intended to leave this world and to ascend into heaven and that all those who would see his face must follow him thither. Then he went up to heaven and prepared a place to which all might come. Then he said, "Hetep sekhet aa," i.e., "Let a great field be produced," and straightway "Sekhet-hetep," or the "Field of Peace," came into being. He next said, "Let there be reeds (aaru) in it," and straightway "Sekhet Aaru," or the "Field of Reeds," came into being. Sekhet-hetep was the Elysian Fields of the Egyptians, and the Field of Reeds was a well-known section of it. Another command of the god Ra resulted in the creation of the stars, which the legend compares to flowers. Then the goddess Nut trembled in all her body, and Ra, fearing that she might fall, caused to come into being the Four Pillars on which the heavens are supported. Turning to Shu, Ra entreated him to protect these supports, and to place himself under Nut, and to hold her up in position with his hands. Thus Shu became the new Sun god in place of Ra, and the heavens in which Ra lived were supported and placed beyond the risk of falling, and mankind would live and rejoice in the light of the new sun.

At this place in the legend, a text is inserted called the "Chapter of the Cow." It describes how the Cow of Heaven and the two Boats of the Sun shall be painted, and gives the positions of the gods who stand by the legs of the Cow, and some short magical names, or formulae, which are inexplicable. The general meaning of the picture of the Cow is quite clear. The Cow represents the sky in which the Boats of Ra, sail, and her four legs are the four cardinal points which cannot be changed. The region above her back is the heaven in which Ra reigns over the beings who pass to there from this earth when they die, and here was situated the home of the gods and the celestial spirits who govern this world.

When Ra had made a heaven for himself and had arranged for a continuance of life on the earth, and the welfare of human beings, he remembered that at one time when reigning on earth he had been bitten by a serpent, and had nearly lost his life through the bite. Fearing that the same calamity might befall his successor, he determined to take steps to destroy the power of all noxious reptiles that dwelt on the earth. With this object in view, he told Thoth to summon Keb, the Earth-god, to his presence, and this god having arrived, Ra told him that war must be made against the serpents that dwelt in his dominions. He further commanded him to go to the god Nu and to tell him to set a watch over all the reptiles that were in the earth and water, and to draw up a writing for every place in which serpents are known to be, containing strict orders that they are to bite, no one. Though these serpents knew that Ra was retiring from the earth, they were never to forget that his rays would fall upon them. In his place, their father Keb was to keep watch over them, and he was their father forever.

As a further protection against them, Ra promised to impart to magicians and snake charmers the particular word of power, hekau, with which he guarded himself against the attacks of serpents, and also to transmit it to his son Osiris. Thus those who are ready to listen to the formulae of the snake charmers shall always be immune from the bites of serpents, and their children also. From this, we may gather that the profession of the snake charmer is very ancient and that this class of magicians was supposed to owe the foundation of their craft to a decree of Ra himself.

Ra next sent for the god Thoth, and when he came into the presence of Ra, he invited him to go with him to a distance, to a place called "Tuat," i.e., hell, or the Other

World, in which region he had determined to make his light to shine. When they arrived there, he told Thoth, the Scribe of Truth, to write down on his tablets the names of all who were therein, and to punish those among them who had sinned against him. He also deputed to Thoth the power to deal absolutely as he pleased with all the beings in the Tuat. Ra loathed the wicked and wished them to be kept at a distance from him. Thoth was to be his vicar, to fill his place, and "Place of Ra," was to be his name. He gave him the power to send out a messenger, so the Ibis came into being. All that Thoth would do would be good, therefore the Tekni bird of Thoth came into being. He gave Thoth power to embrace the heavens, therefore the Moon god came into being. He gave Thoth power to turn back the Northern people, therefore the dog-headed ape of Thoth came into being. Finally, Ra told Thoth that he would take his place in the sight of all those who were wont to worship Ra and that all should praise him as God. Thus the abdication of Ra was complete.

In the fragmentary texts which follow we are told how a man may benefit by the recital of this legend. He must proclaim that the soul which animated Ra was the soul of the Aged One, and then he must proclaim that he is Ra himself, and his word of power Heka. If he recites the Chapter correctly, he shall have life in the Other

World, and he will be held in greater fear there than here. A rubric adds that he must be dressed in new linen garments, and be well washed with Nile water; he must wear white sandals, and his body must be anointed with holy oil. He must burn incense in a censer, and a figure of Maat (Truth) must be painted on his tongue with green paint. These regulations applied to the laity as well as to the clergy.

RA AND ISIS

It has already been seen that the god Ra when retiring from the government of this world, took steps through Thoth to supply mankind with words of power and spells with which to protect themselves against the bites of serpents and other noxious reptiles. The Legend of the Destruction of Mankind affords no explanation of this remarkable fact, but when we read the following legend of Ra and Isis, we understand why Ra, though the king of the gods, was afraid of the reptiles which lived in the kingdom of Keb. The legend, or "Chapter of the Divine God," begins by enumerating the mighty attributes of Ra as the creator of the universe, and describes the god of "many names" as unknowable, even by the gods. At this time, Isis lived in the form of a woman who possessed the knowledge of spells and incantations, that is to say, she was regarded much in the same way as modern African peoples regard their "medicine women," or "witch women." She had used her spells on men and was tired of exercising her powers on them, and she craved the opportunity of making herself mistress of gods and spirits as well as of men. She meditated how she could make herself mistress both of heaven and earth, and finally, she decided that she could only obtain the power she wanted if she possessed the knowledge of the secret name of Ra, in which his very existence was bound up. Ra guarded this name most jealously because he knew that if he revealed it to any being, he would henceforth be at that being's mercy.

Isis saw that it was impossible to make Ra declare his name to her by ordinary methods, and she, therefore, thought out the following plan. It was well known in Egypt and the Sudan at a very early period that if a magician obtained some portion of a person's body, e.g., a hair, a paring of a nail, a fragment of skin, or a portion of some efflux from the body, spells could be used upon them which would have the effect of causing grievous harm to that person. Isis noted that Ra had become old and feeble, and that as he went about, he dribbled at the mouth, and that his saliva fell upon the ground. Watching her opportunity, she caught some of the saliva, and mixing it with dust, she molded it into the form of a large serpent, with poison fangs. And having uttered her spells over it, she left the serpent lying on the path, by which Ra traveled day by day as he went about inspecting Egypt so that it might strike at him as he passed along.

Soon after Isis had placed the serpent on the Path, Ra passed by, and the reptile bit him, thus injecting poison into his body. Its effect was terrible, and Ra cried out in agony. His jaws chattered, his lips trembled, and he became speechless for a time; never before had be suffered such pain. The gods hearing his cry rushed to him, and when he could speak, he told them that a deadly serpent had bitten him. In spite of all the words of power which were known to him, and his secret name which had been hidden in his body at his birth, a serpent had bitten him, and he was being consumed with a fiery pain. He then commanded that all the gods who had any knowledge of magical spells should come to him, and when they came, Isis, the great lady of spells, the destroyer of diseases, and the revivifier of the dead, came with them. Turning to Ra, she said, "What has happened, O divine Father?" and in answer, the god told her that a serpent had bitten him, that he was hotter than fire and colder than water, that his limbs quaked, and that he was losing the power of sight.

Then Isis said to him with guile, "Divine Father, tell me thy name because he who utter his own name shall live."

Thereupon Ra proceeded to enumerate the various things that he had done, and to describe his creative acts and ended his speech to Isis by saying, that he was Khepera in the morning, Ra at noon, and Temu in the evening. Apparently, he thought that the naming of these three great names would satisfy Isis and that she would immediately pronounce a word of power and stop the pain in his body, which, during his speech, had become more acute. Isis, however, was not deceived, and she knew well that Ra had not declared to her his hidden name; this she told him, and she begged him once again to tell her his name. For a time the god refused to utter the name, but as the pain in his body became more violent, and the poison passed through his veins like fire, he said, "Isis shall search in me, and my name shall pass from my body into hers." At that moment Ra removed himself from the sight of the gods in his Boat, and the Throne in the Boat of Millions of Years had no occupant.

The great name of Ra was, it seems, hidden in his heart, and Isis, having some doubt as to whether Ra would keep his word or not, agreed with Horus that Ra must be made to take an oath to part with his two Eyes, that is, the Sun and the Moon. At length, Ra allowed his heart to be taken from his body, and his great and secret name, whereby he lived, passed into the possession of Isis. Ra thus became to all intents and purposes a dead god. Then Isis, strong in the power of her spells, said: "Flow, poison, come out of Ra. Eye of Horus, come out of Ra and shine outside his mouth. It is I, Isis, who work, and I have made the poison to fall on the ground. Truly the name of the great god is taken from him, Ra shall live, and the poison shall die; if the poison live Ra shall die."

This was the spell which was to be used in cases of poisoning, for it rendered the bite or sting of every venomous reptile harmless. It drove the poison out of Ra, and since it was composed by Isis after she obtained the knowledge of his secret name, it was infallible. If the words were written on papyrus or linen over a figure of Temu or Heru-hekenu, or Isis, or Horus, they became a mighty charm. If the papyrus or linen were steeped in water and the water drunk, the words were equally efficacious as a charm against snake bites. To this day, water in which the written words of a text from the Kuran have been dissolved, or water drunk from a bowl on the inside of which religious texts have been written, is still regarded as a never-failing charm in Egypt and the Sudan. Thus we see that the modern custom of drinking magical water was derived from the ancient Egyptians, who believed that it conveyed into their bodies the actual power of their gods.

THE BIRTH OF HORUS, SON OF ISIS AND OSIRIS

The text which contains this legend is found cut in hieroglyphics upon which is now preserved in Paris. Attention was first called to it by Chabas, who in 1857 gave a translation of it in the Revue Archeologique, p. 65 ff., and pointed out the importance of its contents with his characteristic ability. The hieroglyphic text was first published by Ledrain in his work on the monuments of the Bibliotheque Nationale in Paris.

The greater part of the text consists of a hymn to Osiris, which was probably composed under the XVIIIth Dynasty, when an extraordinary development of the cult of that god took place, and when he was placed by Egyptian theologians at the head of all the gods. Though unseen in the temples, his presence filled all Egypt, and his body formed the very substance of the country. He was the God of all gods and the Governor of the Two Companies of the gods, he formed the soul and body of Ra, he was the beneficent Spirit of all spirits, and he was himself the celestial food on which the Doubles in the Other World lived. He was the greatest of the gods in

Heliopolis, Memphis, Herakleopolis, Hermopolis, Abydos, and the region of the First Cataract, and so. He embodied in his own person the might of Ra-Tem, Apis and Ptah, the Horus-gods, Thoth and Khnemu, and his rule over Busiris and Abydos continued to be supreme, as it had been for many, many hundreds of years. He was the source of the Nile, the north wind sprang from him, his seats were the stars of heaven which never set, and the imperishable stars were his ministers. All heaven was his dominion, and the doors of the sky opened before him of their own accord when he appeared. He inherited the earth from his father Keb, and the sovereignty of heaven from his mother Nut. In his person, he united endless time in the past and endless time in the future. Like Ra, he had fought Seba, or Set, the monster of evil, and had defeated him, and his victory assured to him lasting authority over the gods and the dead. He exercised his creative power in making land and water, trees and herbs, cattle and other four-footed beasts, birds of all kinds, and fish and creeping things; even the waste spaces of the desert owed allegiance to him as the creator. And he rolled out the sky and set the light above the darkness.

The last paragraph of the text contains an allusion to Isis, the sister and wife of Osiris, and mentions the legend of the birth of Horus, which even under the XVIIIth

Dynasty was very ancient. Isis, we are told, was the constant protector of her brother, she drove away the demons that wanted to attack him and kept them out of his shrine and tomb, and she guarded him against all accidents. All these things she did using spells and incantations, large numbers of which were known to her, and by her power as the "witch goddess." Her mouth was trained to perfection, and she made no mistake in pronouncing her spells, and her tongue was skilled and halted not. At length came the unlucky day when Set succeeded in killing Osiris during the war which the "good god" was waging against him and his demons. Details of the engagement are wanting, but the Pyramid Texts state that the body of Osiris was hurled to the ground by Set at a place called Netat, which seems to have been near Abydos. The news of the death of Osiris was brought to Isis, and she at once set out to find his body. All legends agree in saying that she took the form of a bird and that she flew about unceasingly, going hither and thither, and uttering wailing cries of grief. At length, she found the body, and with a piercing cry, she alighted on the ground. The Pyramid Texts say that Nephthys, her sister, was with her. The late form of the legend goes on to say that Isis fanned the body with her feathers, and produced air, causing the inert members of Osiris to move, and drew from him his essence, wherefrom she produced her child Horus.

This bare statement of the dogma of the conception of Horus does not represent all that is known about it, and it may well be supplemented by a passage from the Pyramid Texts, which reads:

> *Adoration to thee, O Osiris. Rise thou upon thy left side, place thyself on thy right side. This water which I give unto thee is the water of youth (or rejuvenation). Adoration to thee, O Osiris! Rise thou upon thy left side, place thyself on thy right side. This bread which I have made for thee is warmth. Adoration to thee, O Osiris! The doors of heaven are opened to thee, the doors of the streams are thrown wide open to thee. The gods in the city of Pe come to thee, Osiris, at the sound of the supplication of Isis and Nephthys. Thy elder sister took thy body in her arms; she chafed thy hands, she clasped thee to her breast when she found thee lying on thy side on the plain of Netat.*

And in another place we read:

> *Thy two sisters, Isis and Nephthys, came to thee, Kam-urt, in thy name of Kam-ur, Uatchet-urt, in thy name of Uatch-ur. Isis and Nephthys weave magical protection*

for thee in the city of Saut, in thy name of 'Lord of Saut,'
for their god, in thy name of 'God.' They praise thee; go
not thou far from them in thy name of 'Tua.' They
present offerings to thee; be not wroth in thy name of
'Tchentru.' Thy sister Isis cometh to thee rejoicing in her
love for thee. Thou hast union with her, thy seed entereth
her. She conceiveth in the form of the star Septet (Sothis).
Horus-Sept issueth from thee in the form of Horus,
dweller in the star Septet. Thou makest a spirit to be in
him in his name 'Spirit dwelling in the god Tchentru.'
He avengeth thee in his name of 'Horus, the son who
avenged his father.' Hail, Osiris, Keb hath brought to
thee Horus, he hath avenged thee, he hath brought to thee
the hearts of the gods, Horus hath given thee his Eye, and
thou hast taken possession of the Urert Crown thereby at
the head of the gods. Horus hath presented to thee thy
members, he hath collected them completely, and there is
no disorder in thee. Thoth hath seized thy enemy and
hath slain him and those who were with him.

The above words are addressed to dead kings in the
Pyramid Texts, and what the gods were supposed to do
for them was believed by the Egyptians to have been
actually done for Osiris. These extracts are peculiarly
valuable because they prove that the legend of Osiris

which was current under the XVIIIth Dynasty was based upon traditions which were universally accepted in Egypt under the Vth and VIth Dynasties.

THE DEATH AND RESURRECTION OF HORUS

The magical and religious texts of the Egyptians of all periods contain spells intended to be used against serpents, scorpions, and noxious reptiles of all kinds. Their number and the importance which was attached to them, suggest that Egypt must always have produced these pests in abundance and that the Egyptians were always horribly afraid of them. The text of Unas, which was written towards the close of the Vth Dynasty, contains many such spells. The Theban and Saite Books of the Dead several Chapters consist of nothing but spells and incantations, many of which are based on archaic texts, against crocodiles, serpents, and other deadly reptiles, and insects of all kinds. All such creatures were regarded as incarnations of evil spirits, which attack the dead as well as the living, and therefore it was necessary for the well-being of the former that copies of spells against them, should be written upon the walls of tombs, coffins, funerary amulets, etc.

The gods were just as open to the attacks of venomous reptiles as man, and Ra himself, the king of the gods, nearly died from the poison of a snake bite. Now the gods were, as a rule, able to defend themselves against the attacks of Set and his demons, and the poisonous snakes and insects which were their emissaries. The efforts of Egyptians were directed to the acquisition of a portion of this magical power, which would protect their souls and bodies and their houses and cattle, and other property, each day and each night throughout the year. When a man cared for the protection of himself only, he wore an amulet of some kind, in which the fluid of life was localized. When he wished to protect his house against invasion by venomous reptiles, he placed statues containing the fluid of life in niches in the walls of various chambers, or in some place outside but near the house, or buried them in the earth with their faces turned in the direction from which he expected the attack to come.

Towards the close of the XXVIth Dynasty, when superstition in its most exaggerated form was general in Egypt, it became the custom to make house talismans in the form of small stone stele, with rounded tops, which rested on bases having convex fronts. On the front of such a talisman, was sculptured in relief, a figure of Horus the Child (Harpokrates), standing on two crocodiles, holding in his hands figures of serpents, scorpions, a lion, and a horned animal; each of these being a symbol of an emissary or ally of Set, the god of Evil. Above his head was the head of Bes, and on each side of him were solar symbols, i.e., the lily of Nefer-Tem, figures of Ra and Harmakhis, the Eyes of Ra (the Sun and Moon), etc. The reverse of the stele and the whole of the base were covered with magical texts and spells. When a talisman of this kind was placed in a house, it was supposed to be directly under the protection of Horus and his companion gods, who had vanquished all the hosts of darkness and all the powers of physical and moral evil. Many examples of this talisman are to be seen in the great Museums of Europe, and there are several fine specimens in the Third Egyptian Room in the British Museum. They are usually called "Cippi of Horus." The largest and most important of all these "cippi" is that which is commonly known as the "Metternich Stele," because it was given to Prince Metternich by Muhammad Ali Pasha. It was dug up in 1828 during the building of a cistern in a Franciscan Monastery in Alexandria and was first published with a translation of a large part of the text by Professor Golenischeff. The importance of the stele is enhanced by the fact that it mentions the name of the king in whose reign it was made, viz., Nectanebo I., who reigned from 378 BC to 360 BC.

The obverse, reverse, and two sides of the Metternich Stele have cut upon them nearly three hundred figures of gods and celestial beings. These include figures of the great gods of heaven, earth, and the Other World, figures of the gods of the planets and the Dekans, figures of the gods of the days of the week, of the weeks, and months, and seasons of the year, and of the year. Besides these, there are some figures of local forms of the gods which it is difficult to identify. On the rounded portion of the obverse, the place of honour is held by the solar disk, in which is seen a figure of Khnemu with four ram's heads, which rests between a pair of arms, and is supported on a lake of celestial water. On each side of it are four of the spirits of the dawn, and on the right stands the symbol of the rising sun, Nefer-Temu, and on the left stands Thoth. Below this are five rows of small figures of gods. Below these is Harpokrates in relief, in the attitude already described. He stands on two crocodiles under a kind of canopy, the sides of which are supported by Thoth and Isis, and holds Typhonic animals and reptiles. Above the canopy are the two Eyes of Ra, each having a pair of human arms and hands. On the right of Harpokrates are Seker and Horus, and on his left the symbol of Nefer-

Temu. On the left and right are the goddesses Nekhebet and Uatchet, who guard the South of Egypt and the North respectively. On the reverse and sides are numerous small figures of gods. This stele represented the power to protect man possessed by all the divine beings in the universe, and, however it was placed, it formed an impassable barrier to every spirit of evil and every venomous reptile. The spells, which are cut in hieroglyphics on all the parts of the stele not occupied by figures of gods, were of the most potent character because they contained the actual words by which the gods vanquished the powers of darkness and evil.

The first spell is an incantation directed against reptiles and noxious creatures in general. The chief of these was Apep, the great enemy of Ra, who took the form of a huge serpent that "resembled the intestines," and the spell doomed him to decapitation, and burning and backing in pieces. These things would be effected by Serqet, the Scorpion goddess. The second part of the spell was directed against the poison of Apep and was to be recited over anyone who was bitten by a snake. When uttered by Horus, it made Apep vomit, and when used by a magician properly qualified, would make the bitten person vomit, and so free his body from the poison.

The next spell is directed to be said to the Cat, i.e., a symbol of the daughter of Ra, or Isis, who had the head of Ra, the eyes of the uraeus, the nose of Thoth, the ears of Neb-er-tcher, the mouth of Tem, the neck of Neheb-ka, the breast of Thoth, the heart of Ra, the hands of the gods, the belly of Osiris, the thighs of Menthu, the legs of Khensu, the feet of Amen-Horus, the haunches of Horus, the soles of the feet of Ra, and the bowels of Meh-urit. Every member of the Cat contained a god or goddess, and she was able to destroy the poison of any serpent, or scorpion, or reptile, which might be injected into her body. The spell opens with an address to Ra, who is entreated to come to his daughter, who has been stung by a scorpion on a lonely road and to cause the poison to leave her body. Thus it seems as if Isis, the great magician, was at some time stung by a scorpion.

The next section is very difficult to understand. Ra-Harmakhis is called upon to come to his daughter, and Shu to his wife, and Isis to her sister, who has been poisoned. Then the Aged One, i.e., Ra, is asked to let Thoth turn back Neha-her or Set. "Osiris is in the water, but Horus is with him, and the Great Beetle overshadows him," and every evil spirit which dwells in the water is adjured to allow Horus to proceed to Osiris. Ra, Sekhet, Thoth, and Heka, this last named being the spell personified, are the four great gods who protect Osiris, and who will blind and choke his enemies, and cut out their tongues. The cry of the Cat is again referred to, and Ra is asked if he does not remember the cry which came from the bank of Netit. The allusion here is to the cries which Isis uttered when she arrived at Netit near Abydos and found lying there the dead body of her husband.

At this point on the Stele, the spells are interrupted by a long narrative put into the mouth of Isis, which supplies us with some account of the troubles that she suffered, and describes the death of Horus through the sting of a scorpion. Isis, it seems, was shut up in some dwelling by Set after he murdered Osiris, probably with the intention of forcing her to marry him, and so assist him to legalize his seizure of the kingdom. Isis, as we have already seen, had been made pregnant by her husband after his death, and Thoth now appeared to her, and advised her to hide herself with her unborn child, bringing him forth in secret. He promised her that her son should succeed in due course to his father's throne. With the help of Thoth, she escaped from her captivity and went forth accompanied by the Seven Scorpion goddesses, who brought her to the town of Per-Sui, on the edge of the Reed Swamps. She applied to a woman for a night's shelter, but the woman shut her door in her face. To punish her, one of the Scorpion goddesses forced her way into the woman's house, and stung her child to death. The grief of the woman was so bitter and sympathy-compelling that Isis laid her hands on the child, and, having uttered one of her most potent spells over him, the poison of the scorpion ran out of his body, and the child came to life again. The words of the spell are cut on the Stele, and they were treasured by the Egyptians as an infallible remedy for scorpion stings. When the woman saw that her son had been brought back to life by Isis, she was filled with joy and gratitude. And, as a mark of her repentance, she brought large quantities of things from her house as gifts for Isis, and they were so many that they filled the house of the kind but poor woman, who had given Isis shelter.

Now soon after Isis had restored to life the son of the woman who had shown churlishness to her, a terrible calamity fell upon her because her beloved son Horus was stung by a scorpion and died. The news of this event was conveyed to her by the gods, who cried out to her to come to see her son Horus, whom the terrible scorpion Uhat had killed. Isis, stabbed with pain at the news, as if a knife had been driven into her body, ran out distraught with grief. It seems that she had gone to perform a religious ceremony in honour of Osiris in a temple near Hetep-hemt, leaving her child carefully concealed in Sekhet-An. During her absence, the scorpion Uhat, which had been sent by Set, forced its way into the biding place of Horus and there stung him to death. When Isis came and found the dead body, she burst forth in lamentations, the sound of which brought all the people from the neighboring districts to her side. As she related to them the history of her sufferings, they endeavored to console her, and when they found this to be impossible, they lifted up their voices and wept with her. Then Isis placed her nose in the mouth of Horus so that she might discover if he still breathed, but there was no breath in his throat, and when she examined the wound in his body made by the demon Aun-Ab, she saw in it traces of poison. No doubt about his death then remained in her mind, and clasping him in her arms she lifted him up, and in her transports of grief leaped about like fish when they are laid on red-hot coals. Then she uttered a series of heartbreaking laments, each of which begins with the words "Horus is bitten." The heir of heaven, the son of Un- Nefer, the child of the gods, he who was wholly fair, is bitten! He for whose wants I provided, he who was to avenge his father, is bitten! He for whom I cared and suffered when he was being fashioned in my womb, is bitten! He whom I tended so that I might gaze upon him, is bitten! He whose life I prayed for, is bitten! Calamity has overtaken the child, and he has perished".

While Isis was saying these and many similar words, her sister Nephthys, who had been weeping bitterly for her nephew Horus as she wandered about among the swamps, came, in company with the Scorpion-goddess Serqet, and advised Isis to pray to heaven for help. Pray that the sailors in the Boat of Ra may cease from rowing because the Boat cannot travel onwards while Horus lies dead. Then Isis cried out to heaven, and her voice reached the Boat of Millions of Years, and the Disk ceased to move onward and came to a standstill. From the Boat Thoth descended, being equipped with words of power and spells of all kinds, and bearing with him the "great command of maa-kheru," i.e., the WORD. Then he came to Isis and told her that no harm could possibly have happened to Horus because he was under the protection of the Boat of Ra; but his words failed to comfort Isis, and though she acknowledged the greatness of his designs, she complained that they savored of delay. "What is the good," she asks, "of all your spells, and incantations, and magical formulae, and the great command of maa-kheru, if Horus is to perish by the poison of a scorpion, and to lie here in the arms of Death? Evil, evil is his destiny".

In answer to these words Thoth, turning to Isis and Nephthys, bade them to fear not, and to have no anxiety about Horus because, said he, "I have come from heaven to heal the child for his mother." He then pointed out that Horus was under protection as the Dweller in his Disk (Aten), the Great Dwarf, the Mighty Ram, the Great Hawk, the Holy Beetle, the Hidden Body, the Divine Bennu, etc., and proceeded to utter the great spell which restored Horus to life. By his words of power Thoth transferred the fluid of life of Ra, and as soon as this came upon the child's body the poison of the scorpion flowed out of him, and he once more breathed and lived. When this was done, Thoth returned to the Boat of Ra, the gods who formed its crew resumed their rowing, and the Disk passed on its way to make its daily journey across the sky. The gods in heaven, who were amazed and uttered cries of terror when they heard of the death of Horus, were made happy once more and sang songs of joy over his recovery. The happiness of Isis in her child's restoration to life was very great because she could again hope that he would avenge his father's murder, and occupy his throne. The final words of Thoth comforted her greatly. He told her that he would take charge of the case of Horus in the Judgment Hall of Anu, wherein Osiris had been judged. Furthermore, he would give Horus power to repulse any attacks which might be made upon him by beings in the heights above or demons in the depths below, and would ensure his succession to the Throne of the Two Lands, i.e., Egypt. Thoth also promised Isis that Ra himself should act as the advocate of Horus, even as he had done for his father Osiris. He was also careful to allude to the share which Isis had taken in the restoration of Horus to life, saying, "It is the words of power of his mother which have lifted up his face, and they shall enable him to journey wheresoever he pleases, and to put fear into the powers above. I myself hasten to obey them." Thus everything turned on the power of the spells of Isis, who made the sun to stand still and caused the dead to be raised.

Such are the contents of the texts on the famous Metternich Stele. There appears to be some confusion in their arrangement, and some of them clearly are misplaced, and, in places, the text is manifestly corrupt. It is impossible to explain several passages since we do not understand all the details of the system of magic which they represent. Still, the general meaning of the texts on the Stele is quite clear, and they record a legend of Isis and Horus which is not found so fully described on any other monument.

ISIS AND OSIRIS

The history of Isis and Osiris is taken from the famous treatise of Plutarch entitled De Iside et Osiride. It contains all the essential facts given in Plutarch's work, and the only things omitted are his derivations and mythological speculations, which are really unimportant for the Egyptologist. Egyptian literature is full of allusions to events which took place in the life of Osiris, and to his persecution, murder, and resurrection, and numerous texts of all periods describe the love and devotion of his sister and wife Isis, and the filial piety of Horus. Nowhere, however, have we in Egyptian a connected account of the causes which led to the murder by Set of Osiris, or of the subsequent events which resulted in his becoming the king of heaven and judge of the dead. However, carefully we piece together the fragments of information which we can extract from native Egyptian literature, there still remains a series of gaps which can only be filled by guesswork. Plutarch, as a learned man and a student of comparative religion and mythology, was most anxious to understand the history of Isis and Osiris, which Greek and Roman scholars talked about freely, and which none of them comprehended. He made inquiries of priests and others and examined critically such information as he could obtain, believing and hoping that he would penetrate the mystery in which these gods were wrapped. As a result of his labors, he collected a number of facts about the form of the Legend of Isis and Osiris as it was known to the learned men of his day. But there is no evidence that he had the slightest knowledge of the details of the original African Legend of these gods as it was known to the Egyptians, under the VIth Dynasty. Moreover, he never realized that the characteristics and attributes of both Isis and Osiris changed several times during the long history of Egypt and that a thousand years before he lived, the Egyptians themselves had forgotten what the original form of the legend was. They preserved some ceremonies and performed very carefully all the details of an ancient ritual at the annual commemoration festival of Osiris which was held in November and December, but the evidence of the texts makes it quite clear that the meaning and symbolism of nearly all the details were unknown alike to priests and people.

An important modification of the cult of Isis and Osiris took place in the third century before Christ, when the Ptolemies began to consolidate their rule in Egypt. A form of religion which would be acceptable both to Egyptians and Greeks had to be provided, and this was produced by modifying the characteristics of Osiris and calling him Sarapis and identifying him with the Greek

Pluto. To Isis, were added many of the attributes of the great Greek goddesses, and into her worship were introduced "mysteries" derived from non-Egyptian cults, which made it acceptable to the people everywhere. Had a high priest of Osiris, who lived at Abydos under the XVIIIth Dynasty, witnessed the celebration of the great festival of Isis and Osiris in any large town in the first century before Christ, it is certain that he would have regarded it as a lengthy act of worship of strange gods, in which there appeared, here and there, ceremonies and phrases which reminded him of the ancient Abydos ritual. When the form of the cult of Isis and Osiris introduced by the Ptolemies into Egypt extended to the great cities of Greece and Italy, still further modifications took place in it, and the characters of Isis and Osiris were still further changed. By degrees, Osiris came to be regarded as the god of death pure and simple, or as the personification of Death, and he ceased to be regarded as the great protecting ancestral spirit, and the all-powerful protecting Father of his people.

As the importance of Osiris declined that of Isis grew, and men came to regard her as the great Mother goddess of the world. The priests described from tradition the great facts of her life according to the Egyptian legends. How she had been a loving wife; how she had gone forth after her husband's murder by Set to seek for his body; how she had found it and revived it by her spells and had union with Osiris, and conceived by him, her son, in pain and loneliness in the Swamps of the Delta; how she watched over him until he was old enough to fight and vanquish his father's murderer, and how she seated him in triumph on his father's throne. These things endeared Isis to the people everywhere, and as she herself had not suffered death like Osiris, she came to be regarded as the eternal mother of life and all living things. She was the creatress of crops; she produced fruit, vegetables, plants of all kinds and trees, she made cattle prolific, she brought men and women together and gave them offspring, she was the authoress of all love, virtue, goodness and happiness. She made the light to shine, and she was the spirit of the Dog-star which heralded the Nile-flood. She was also the source of the power in the beneficent light of the moon; and finally, she took the dead to her bosom and gave them peace, and introduced them to a life of immortality and happiness similar to that which she had bestowed upon Osiris.

The message of the cult of Isis as preached by her priests, was one of hope and happiness. And coming to the Greeks and Romans, as it did, at a time when men were weary of their national cults, and when the speculations of the philosophers carried no weight with the general public, the people everywhere welcomed it with the greatest enthusiasm. From Egypt, it was carried to the Islands of Greece and the mainland, to Italy, Germany, France, Spain and Portugal, and then crossing the western end of the Mediterranean it entered North Africa, and with Carthage as a center, spread east and west along the coast. Wherever the cult of Isis came, men accepted it as something which supplied what they thought to be lacking in their native cults. Rich and poor, gentle and simple, all welcomed it, and the philosopher, as well as the ignorant man, rejoiced in the hope of a future life which it gave to them. Its Egyptian origin caused it to be regarded with the most profound interest. Its priests were most careful to make the temples of Isis quite different from those of the national gods, and to decorate them with obelisks, sphinxes, shrines, altars, etc., which were either imported from temples in Egypt or were copied from Egyptian originals.

In the temples of Isis, services were held at daybreak and in the early afternoon daily, and everywhere these were attended by crowds of people. The holy water used in the libations and for sprinkling the people was Nile water, specially imported from Egypt, and to the votaries of the goddess, it symbolized the seed of the god

Osiris, which germinated and brought forth fruit through the spells of the goddess Isis. The festivals and processions of Isis were everywhere most popular and were enjoyed by learned and unlearned alike. In fact, the Isis play which was acted annually in November, and the festival of the blessing of the ship, which took place in the spring, were the most important festivals of the year. Curiously enough, all the oldest gods and goddesses of Egypt, with the exception of Osiris, Isis, Anubis, and Harpokrates that for several hundreds of years were the principal objects of worship of some of the most cultured and intellectual nations, passed into absolute oblivion. The treatise of Plutarch De Iside helps to explain how this came about, and for those who study the Egyptian Legend of Isis and Osiris, the work has considerable importance.

BIBLIOGRAPHY

Klingensmith, Annie. *Stories of Norse Gods and Heroes.* Chicago: A. Flanagan, 1894.

H. Harding, Caroline. *Stories of Greek Gods, Heroes and Men.* Chicago: Foresman and Company, 1897.

Wallis Budge, E. A. *Legends of the Gods.* London: British Museum, 1912.

16591999R00072

Printed in Great Britain
by Amazon